A

Night Creature

Trilogy

The

Sleepless Night Creature

By

HDA Pratt

Acknowledgements

Firstly I would like to start my thank you off with the man who said yes to marrying me, my Karl. Even though you have never and probably will never read a thing I have written, I know you would be my most honest critic and I thank you for not tearing my heart out with your honesty. I love our family and the bubble we have made for ourselves, a safe and warm place for me to forever do my writings. If we ever find ourselves as the creatures in this book, immortal, I know I enjoy eternity because it will be with you. Next I would like to thank the parental's of course, for the encouragement and love I receive from you both every day. The faith you have in me and my dreams will truly keep me going with whatever path life leads me on. I also want to thank my big sister Fiona for without you, I would not have my scary movie buddy to watch all the horror's with. Thanking my Chester and Daisy, the love your two daddies have for you is so big I cannot describe it, even as a self-published author. Lastly I would like to thank Stuart Tricker for being my over worked editor, even though you never asked for the job! Having your opinions on my little worlds has made the clarity I need to see from time to time as a writer so thank you.

One

A drink in his hand, the golden liquid catches the candle light just right for his eyes to sparkle. Bloodshot, the individual veins circling his grey iris like they are going to take over. Hungry to break free, I catch a glimpse of his ulnar artery pumping on over drive as he necks back the rest of his whisky.

Darting to the left, he slightly trips going for his prey. His overexcitement at seeing one of the least unusual looking whores in this house burns through him, his need to escape the family life he has made at home crying out. How funny it is to watch these pathetic creatures hunt and mourn the fact that they have grown a family, married like they are told to but then spend any night they can getting their rocks off with someone else. Chuckling to myself I see a young looking whore eye me up for the corner, thinking I am here waiting for the same need as these gentlemen.

Stepping back further into the corner I have situated myself in, the candle next to me dims as I push my un-holiness into the area around me. Not phased by the candle seeming to shrink and the shadows growing to hide me more, the girl talks to a gentleman just in front of me, her eyes never leaving my position.

Ignoring her for a moment I check on my drunken prey, his struggle to get what he wants is painful at best. How he is planning on getting his rocks off, when from the look of him I do not believe he is even going to get to her before he passes out. Nicely dressed he looks to have come from a party of some kind, his maroon tail coats flap behind him as he nearly jumps over a passed out boy on the floor, way too young to be here. Hand in the air, he still carries his empty glass, his ginger hair slicked back tight against his head with the greasiest substance I'm sure he could find.

Focusing my hearing on him alone I hear every heavy breath he puffs, feel his heart pounding on overdrive as he nearly kills his body from all the alcohol and need for more of it. Muttering, he stammers a single word over and over and over again, hoping that she will finally turn from the hunk of rock, the beast of a gentleman who's lap the whore is sat upon. Why do they do this to themselves, piss each other off and wonder why they fight. All of them do it, even in small way sometimes, but if humans would just leave each other alone all these pointless wars they drag themselves into would never happen.

Take now for instance, there are twelve not bad looking whores waiting on the stairs, ready for some work. A quiet night it seems, or I am too early to have come here for the crowd of visitors; my prey could easily get with one of those whores. Why the need to go after one that has already found herself her own prey. At least wait another two hours and you can have her like she is a new flower ready for him alone.

Chuckling to myself again, my frozen heart jumps a beat as the girl I totally forgot about appears by my side.

"Alraght sar" Her country twinge of an accent drools at me.

"It's sir" I correct

"Sorray"

Still not looking her way, I pull the darkness further down around us, my own hunger beginning to set in as I have not eaten for weeks. Why, well I wanted to save up for one big evening of over indulgence. Finding a library deep within the city where I could stay and read all day and night, I relished the chance. After the kind librarian showed me to the section I was interested in, I feed. Feed my need of knowledge, of taking everything I could get from all the books laid before me. Though now, the blood pumping through all of the warm blooded creatures calls for me to feed, and feed deep.

"How's yar evening gone? You look a little lonely and lost over har" Listening carefully, I can't help but break down the way she over pronounces the words she's saying wrongly.

"Har?" I quiz wanting to check one last time.

"Don't like ow I speak sar?" She utter, pushing everything she has into keeping her odd twinge up.

Turning to her in a flash of movement, her eyes go wide as I give her my full focus. Pretty, I wonder if she must have slipped through my man's drunken gaze and she is on a different level to every other whore here. Pale of course, just like most of the girls in this wet country of ours. Her eyes are a deep brown, while her hair is touched by the sun. Golden and grown down to her breasts, her corset pushes her handful up nicely enough that any man's eyes could get lost in them. Her dress looking to be of a higher quality than the rest of the girls in here, I arch my eyebrow at her as my eyes delve into hers.

Flashes of pink and baby blue, her mind takes me into a bright white room with Victorian bay windows taking up the whole left side. Finery and elegance scream from every piece of hand crafted furniture in the room, as a maid gives a little boy on the floor a bottle to have. Wearing the baby blue I saw, a woman frozen onto her seat in the corner, looks just like the girl only ten years older. On her lap in a bright pink dress is a young blond girl giggling at the way her dolls hair has curled.

Pulling myself out of her mind, the glazed overlook the girl's eyes beam; begin to wash away as I uncurl my grip on her mind. Not seeing a thing I saw, she breaks her façade and lets her over educated self-free for a moment.

"What on this godly earth just happened?" Her eyes going wide again, she takes a step back only to find the other side of the corner I am next to. "I meeen sar, wat jist happan?"

"Too late young Claire, I know your secret." I whisper right in her ear, pushing my voice to sail to her through the space between us.

Shocked again, her eyes widen as she really takes me in. My whiter than white skin, my own copper hair is grown down to my shoulders, perfectly cut into a design to make me more alluring. A beard lightly sprinkling my face makes any one who sees me look at my lips, a beautiful firm set ready to kiss anyone. Eyes green, they shine like no eyes should, a light coming from the pupils as I look out into this world. A manly set jaw and strong cheekbones, I do not let fear grow into people when they see me from afar. But up close, when my fangs come out and the darkness swims around me, fear they never knew they could feel consumes them.

How I know I look this way, well my lover over a hundred years ago kindly and soothing told me. He explained everything about the way I am and the way I look since I cannot look in a mirror anymore. Hungry to see what he saw, I delved into his mind and soaked up everything I saw there. Wanting what I saw I made the mistake of turning him, making him what I was, only to be so drawn into him and his eyes that I drunk him dry. The pain of being a night creature, of being undead, well a vampire, I would have some sorrow in my history, otherwise how would I live so lonely for so long.

"Do not fear me my girl" I tell her bringing myself back to this pretty thing. Placing my hand on her forearm, I let the darkness I placed over our corner leave, returning the candle back to its original brightness.

Feeling her breath lessen, her eyes having dropped, she raises them back up to me. Her curiousness overtaking the fear that spun in her two seconds before, she lets her fake accent disappear. Who she truly is finds me, as her back straightens and she stands like the proud elitist that she is.

"I pray-tell, what are you sir?

"Me? Just a creature looking for some food, for some warmth in the day to come" Giving her a smile I turn back to the room.

"And I am not good enough?" Sounding sad, I release my hold on her forearm but instead signal for her to join me at a table in front of us.

"My child do not be sad, it is a good thing you have not drawn my interest for tonight. Yes I do give you that you are desirable, but tonight my interest has been taken by another." Hand in the air, I signal to the bartender for two drinks.

"Oh. My mother said I was always second; always second to win a school prize, always second to win a man's heart. Never the best but never the worst was my father's counter."

"Where are your parents? You are say, eighteen rotations of the sun?"

"What a funny way to say it, though I guess you are right. My parents left me. Moved their whole family to Wales, a new house awaiting them on a beautiful hillside. I stayed, having fallen head over heels for a boy, thinking we would be married by the end of the year and I would be head of our household. We would have maids and butlers that would cater to my every need while he worked and slowly took over his father's law firm." Her voice stopping as the barman set down two scotches, the same as I ordered when I first arrived.

Nodding he waits for money, expecting that as he brought them over that he would get a tip. Turning my eyes on him, I command him to leave through my thoughts alone, his mind already falling under my control when I spoke with him earlier.

"You haven't paid." She comments, still clearly catching up with me not being an everyday patron in this delightful establishment.

"I do not need to"

"You own this place? I thought Josepha did"

"I do not own this place, I just have a way with people now… What are we going to do with you?" I ask, my full attention now on her.

"What do you mean?" She puzzles, clearly a little afraid.

"Let's begin with his name?"

"Who? Clive" I nod, seeing that she is getting there. "His name is Clive Johnston Ashwood. He lives on Ashwood Street by the fountain in the estate there. The manor that was meant to be mine before that slut Cassandra came in and took first prize. Like I said to you, I am always second, always."

"Firstly, the whinnying will seize immediately. Women have always been taught and teach themselves that you are the inferior sex, the lower being who will do what her husband tells her. I tell you Claire… you are not the inferior. In fact there is a reason men try to keep your sex down. You are higher than them." I state believing what I say, excluding me of course. "Now do you like your name?"

"My name? Claire, you mean… wait you're confusing me. Why do you keep asking me these questions?" Picking up her whisky for her, I place it in her hand.

"Drink and answer my questions. Where we go next will depend on your answers"

Swigging it down in one movement, I have a feeling she does this every night before having to go out into this house and find a client. The poor girl, all of these girls in-fact, but I know I can only help one of them, if she wants it. If she seizes it.

"Your name?"

"I am Claire Francis De'Lucatin and I hate my name. Hate the woman my mother has made me into. Hate that this is now my life, because of men, because of Clive Ashwood." Anger spilling from her, I feel her heart pounding, her hate for her mother becoming real. Burning like a coal fire deep in her chest ready to let her heat burn the next person that puts her down.

Good.

"Would you like a new name?" I ask, her eyes looking at mine.

"A new start..." I say slowly finishing my questions with my last question. "A new life?"

Dipping her head, she reaches out for my drink, taking it in her hand before bring the glass slowly to her lips. Whispering, I know she's finally getting it, getting that I am not normal. Not human.

"Yes... I am ready for it to begin" Tipping my scotch back, her eyes light up as her freedom from this life is open to her. The joy that is filling her shines brighter than my eyes could even try to. Tonight this girl will die, but she will die happy.

Sliding my key over the table, just like any of the clients in here do with their whores, I give her my room number and tell her to wait for me there.

"I will meet you soon. I must finish my hunt, feed so I cannot feed no more." Locking eyes with her, I show my fangs, making it as clear to her as I can "Your life will change forever" Walking past me, she flicks my hair, already much more confident in who she is. If anyone deserves to become undead it is someone like her, someone seizing the night.

With Claire now gone I scour the room once again, looking for my next prey. Busier than it was before, I see now that only two whore still wait on the steps, every man in the room having a whore around his neck. Ignoring me after seeing me give Claire my key, the whores make it easy for me to scour the room.

To my delight, the dirt covered walls show my marron suited man has only just made it to the hunk of rock and the plain Jane on his lap. Watching the scene unfold, I laugh as he thinks he's being suave when he bumps into them. Instead, his deep heavy breathing and sweat covered lump of a body knocks the whore so she falls off the hunks lap and he falls into her place. As drunk as the marron suited man, the hunk doesn't even notice that they've swapped places and moves in to kiss his new whore.

Stopping him, the plain Jane smiles at both of the men. Focusing my hearing on her, I hear the words clear as day, wondering if she offers this service a lot. "How about both ya men comes with me and we all have a great time?" Her twinge of an accent truly being hers, it seems to do the trick for both men.

Standing up, the hunk brings the marron suited man up with him. Being far sturdier on his feet than his new ginger lover, the rock carries him as the whore leads them down a side corridor next to the stairway. Laughing to myself, I think how convenient that this woman has just added herself and the hunk of rock to my meal. Gorging myself after the weeks of no food, this is something I will definitely not be turning down.

Following easily I sulk past all the busy cliental of the house, some seeming to find it hard to wait till they find a room from the look of the tents in their trouser. Sending a quick laugh into the ear of the last man I pass, he jumps up pushing the young lady off his lap. Giving him a confused look, the girl moves off to another potential client, not wanting to get mixed up with a man who's a little too rough.

Leaving the main room, I find myself in a tightly spaced corridor, the lighting in here darker than I even make it when hunting someone. Clearly one of the cheaper rooms in this fine establishment, the doorways only have half ripped bed sheets as doors. Noises that any high class mother would never want to be hearing escape the sheets as I pass. Using my sense of smell, I slowly make my way down a set of tightly built in steps taking me further into darkness.

Covering himself in ginger and pine scents, the marron suited man is not hard to track. His whore on the other-hand gives off the same smell as every girl in this place, all of them living in close quarters, washing only when they can find a mildly clean source of water. Knowing from this tiny fact that Claire is of much tougher meat than her parents made out, any high elite could never dream of living like this.

Lights completely gone, the basement level is far bigger than the building above. Buying out the space from the other houses circling this one, this new space tells me the ruler of this house knows many people on this saddened street would rather make a quick buck selling the cold part of their homes they never use. After all, what better thing to have in your basement than a raging sex haven of dirt and disease or a spare room for all the items you do not own to fill up the place. Doors back on the frames down here; I see the benefit of having unused space from other houses means you get to keep the doors that came with them.

Turning left, then right, it is much more of a maze down here; the smell of the ginger man fills my nose as I savour the goal waiting ahead. Quieter and empty, I assume the rooms down here will fill up as the clients above begin to show real eagerness to get going.

Taking a final right, I feel a slight hold of my hunger as the young whore waits outside a room alone. Door closed next to her, I wait using my heightened sense of hearing to make out the noises in the room behind. Closed, it makes me so confused for a moment. I was excepting to find her on the bed, the men waiting to begin the offer she gave them. Instead it looks as if she has been ousted herself.

Flashing to her side in a single breath, her next breath is used up by the intake she has from me suddenly appearing. "Hello miss"

"Sar" She coughs out, her shock of me disappearing as she sees my alluring eyes. Seeing where Claire has taken her choice of words from, I ask the question biting at my lips.

"The gentlemen you came down here with, where did they go?"

"Why? You a pig? They an't don noting wrong" She huffs, my allure losing its power quickly. Whatever she feels for these men is strong; meaning her protectiveness for them is something I cannot compete with.

"It's just I overheard you offer them both your service and now you out here. A door behind you is closed shut and noises are coming from inside." I point out, closing the space between us. "I am definitely no pig. A bat maybe"

"A bat? Tat's a weird choice of animal. Anyhows, the two men you ask'd about are in ere. Alone, if you know what I mean" Wiggling her eyebrows, her once cute smile looks me up and down. "You though I feel, is a watcher" Saying her last words harshly right up to my lips, I smile bringing my lips apart to reveal my white diamonds pointing out and ready.

Her eyes shooting large, I seep into her mind looking for an explanation to the familiarity she has with these men.

Green and purple velvet is all I get at first, mixed with the deep dirty brown of her dress. Unfolding before me, a scene fills my vision, this woman's mind is doing all it can to fight me. Two men, like before only one sits behind a big desk, the hunk standing behind him with a hand on his shoulder.

The hunk wearing the green, the other the purple, I see this unfortunate plain girl on a single chair in front of the ginger ones desk. Cleaned up a bit too much for the accent she presents the world, I have a feeling these men are they reason she looks cleaner, the scene I'm viewing is a new meeting between the three of them.

"So it's agreed. We will pay you twenty bucks a night and you move in with Arnold as his sister. For this you pretend to invite us frequently to have alone time with the both of us at the whore house we have saved you from, only for you to wait while we ourselves secretly make love?" Raising his eyebrow like he is talking to a tiny child, the ginger man is everything I thought he would be. Harsh, rude and actually quite clever in his own right, the arrogance coming off of him as his golden wedding ring catches his desk candles light showing his infertility. This ginger one is a perfect meal for me after my, self-made, hunger strike, his higher and self-righteous attitude is one I love to see scared as I feed their life away.

"Twenty bucks! God ya"

Cutting her reply off I pull out of her mind, this arrangement makes everything that has confused me logical. Of course her standing outside would usually be weird but now....

Her pale grey eyes are coming back into sight, I don't let her confusion of having me in her mind wash off. Instead, I go straight for my food source. My left hand on the side of her head, I use my right to pin her shoulder in place as I bite down hard on her artery.

Blood spurting out across the wall in a rush of escaping red, I don't keep this kill clean. My hunger taking control, I let it feed on everything it can, biting her more than once to make the blood escape into my awaiting mouth. Guzzling, my usually far quieter dinner time is taken over by the need to have her blood now.

Drinking till my heart is full of warmth pounding into my body, I feel the blood soaking into my everything, driven by the hunger that is taking over. Throwing her empty life to the side the craving hunger still burning inside me takes control. Bashing in the doorway with an overdramatic kick that wasn't needed, the two men lay lovingly in each other's embrace.

Deeper than I thought, when I delved into the mind trance, it seems it must have taken a long time. With weeks of no blood and only just feeding on Claire, it is not a surprise so much time has passed. The off white shirt I wear is deeply covered in blood, as is my face.

Startled awake, the two men look at me flabbergasted for a moment. Who am I and why have I kick the door in. Knowing their first thought is the same as the girl, could I be a pig, I smile my fangs at them. Certainly not with all the blood covering me, I answer for them in my own head. Diving forward I give them no time to escape or even a chance to think of what is happening. Tonight is when these two are going to die and after their last love session I feel it isn't a bad time to go.

Going for Arnold first, I slice my sharp dagger pointed nail along his overly muscled throat, his blood spurting out over me as I cut too deeply. Crying out for his dying love, the ginger one moves to jump to his naked feet, the dirty bed sheets giving him a rash on his left side.

Grabbing him by the arm, I yank him back next to his lover as I feed deeply, the horror of my hunger scaring him so much no sound comes out of his mouth. Tasting better than their whore outside, my body always shivers from the next intake of blood it has been seeking. The hunks' blood pouring out into my mouth, I lick up as much as I can, letting the deep red substance feed my soul.

Stopping my gorge half way, I put the marron suited man out of his misery and bite down into the wrist of the man. Having wanted him all night to feed upon, his blood tastes the best, the hunt I had placed on him when I first saw him entering this house of disgusting smells, making my body beg for all of his blood.

Pure and heavenly, the blood that pours out of his wrist tingles on my tongue as it fills my mouth. Not letting any escape as I had with my last two victims, I saviour all of it, his scream of pain taking over the fear that I have killed his lover. Covering his mouth with my hand not on his wrist, I do not want someone coming to find me mid meal. Living off the pain I feel shaking throughout his body, I drink deeper taking all the blood I can get.

Drinker harder and faster, his body soon relaxes as every ounce of blood flowing in him seeps into me. My hunger vanishing easily now, I let his arm go as I quickly finish off Arnold. Over indulging myself for certain, I have quickly fed more than I will need for another week. Letting myself grow this hungery, it's amazing I didn't feed on the entire upstairs room before I made it down to the basement.

Deep red and dark marron colours now cover every dirty beige thing in this room and hallway. Telling myself off for letting the hunger get out of control, I slide off the bed to see how much mess I have truly made. Keeping your feedings, unless you are at home, to a calm pace usually means a small clean up. Tonight I have made my own little hell for anyone to see, for anyone to catch. Knowing I have Claire still waiting upstairs for me, I use my new absorbed life blood and get to cleaning up quickly. Being caught by another whore and her client is not needed tonight.

Two

Bodies and blood gone, I flash quickly up through the whore house, the grubbiness of the place being made worse by the sweat now in the rooms. Passing all the clients and their girls without anyone seeing, I head up the half broken stairs and move straight for my newly rented room for the night.

Slipping inside quickly, Claire takes a moment before realising I have even entered. Screaming horror at the sight of me, the single flickering candle next to the window makes the blood on my shirt and mouth dance shadows across the nicely decorated rooms of the higher levels. Being a whore house no one comes to her rescue, girls screaming here is clearly a regular occurrence. Velvet and satin, it confuses me as to why my victims didn't pay for a room like this. They clearly had the money but maybe waiting outside a room up here is way odder than down in the basement.

Red, the colour of us night creatures, whores and vampires, this room has red everywhere. The curtains with gold trimmings hang down to the candle at the window, setting the scene for any sexy woman dancing before a customer. The dark tinted wooden floor, painted red to match the bedding, hides the drops of wet blood coming off my shirt. Glad Claire cannot see this; I tear off my shirt and wipe my face with it.

Moving off to the right, a golden bowl, painted with a cheap flaking paint, waits for me to have a quick rinse. Leaving

Claire with a questioning look on her face from my strip show, I clean up fast, pulling my long hair up into a tight ponytail.

"Where on earth have you been? It's nearly morning. I thought you had let me come up here just to have a nice sleep. All that talk of becoming someone new was a joke. And now you somehow appear in the room without the door opening and are covered in blood. What's going on? You said I wasn't drawing your interest. What about now that we are alone. Am I next to help you end up covered in blood? My Blood?" Seeming to decide whether she should try running for it or just let her own death happen, I see the conflict happening inside her.

"Calm yourself girl. I will explain all to you, but first did you decide on a name?" Taking off my shoes, I move to the closet where I put some items earlier in the evening.

"Name? I thought I was just forgetting mine" Watching me move about the room, I feel her eyes burning into the scars running down the whole of my back.

"Yes you will no longer be the naive Claire you once were. After tonight you will become braver, stronger and more powerful than any man before you could hope to be. But you shall still need a name." Unhooking my cloak from its hanger, the white fabric sizzles against my fingertips, the velvet reacting to my skin. Pulling it on, I do up all the small buttons running down the inside, sealing my naked flesh from her eyes.

"Do I have to decide now? Am I getting a cloak like that?"

Chuckling at her eagerness, I hope she is truly ready for this. Her transition will not be anywhere near as bad as mine was but, becoming undead is always a strain on the body. We are undead of course, so no sunlight, no mirrors and definitely no life, in a way anyway.

"Any ideas on what you might… enjoy as your name?"

"I feel I only want one name. No first or last, just one. Something solid, cold or at least strong"

Moving across the room I nod at her, understanding the need to lose a last name. After all, the only reason women have them is because men decided they have to be owned by them. Take this Ashwood fellow, his father has the whole street named after them, just so he can mark his territory, like a dog.

"What is your name? I've been telling you all about me, but what about you? What was your name before?" Arching my eyebrow at her, I beg her pardon without saying the words.

"I mean, at least what is your name now" Shuffling on the bed slightly, I hear every ripple of the hay, stuffed in the cheap bed she is on. Wondering if I should take her to mine for this transformation, I think again. Knowing my plan of action, being here in town, is the best place for this.

"Cayden McNigh" I say. No emotion, no feeling coming along with it. "I will tell you my first name, but not today."

"Cayden" She whispers, thinking I cannot hear her. "McNigh, that sounds welsh or Scottish"

"I do not know. I must have read it somewhere before I became what I am now. But I felt the name, felt it was me. I have been Cayden McNigh for over three hundred years and I will always be Cayden McNigh" Her eyes, turning to slits, size me up seeing if what I say is a lie. Even after everything she has witnessed, everything I have asked of her. She is still wondering deep down if this is all a game for me, all something she is working the night for.

"Three hundred years. That's not possible, not even for someone as strange as you"

Pulling her to her feet, I flash before her, moving the room around so all the furniture is squashed up against the walls. The bed lifted up against the wall, I have moved the dusty matt off the floor, rolling it up next to the window. Flashing so quickly the awaiting dust puffs up everywhere I move. Seeing how dirty these rooms are means making the mess will not be much of a problem.

"You know just what I am… now your name please" I utter sternly, moving back in front of her. Her heart beating on overdrive, I feel her excitement at all this, of seeing me move so quickly, of seeing that I truly am what she thinks I am. A vampire.

"I think… I believe I want to be called." Closing her eyes, her chest heaves up as she takes in a deep hard breath. Falling into her own mind, just like I did all the years ago, I feel the name she is going to give me comes from her soul. Her true name, the name she has meant to be this whole short life of hers.

"Eferhild"

"Warrior Maiden" I whisper, knowing this name from the history books I have invested so much time in. "The last known Eferhild in recorded history was a maiden made to fight a bear with her own two hands. Forced into a forest where a brown bear and her cubs waited, the maiden only had one choice. Meet this bear and win. Above all odds, Eferhild won, but rather than killing the bear and its cubs, she brought the bear on her side by a show of strength. The King, who forced her into the forest for his own amusement, died at the hands of all the bears now under Eferhild's control." Telling her the legend of her own choice of name, I feel she knows this already, by the proud look across her lips. "I must say a fine choice you have made."

Grabbing the front of her dress, her smile vanishes as I rip the old faded fabric off her with utter ease. Her under garments the only items remaining on her, she looks raw and ready.

Shocked and hurt in my act, she moves to slap me, I let her get the hit in. Sharp and stinging, her hand moves away from my hardened face, the pain I should feel if I was human means she will make a very strong fighter.

"Tonight you will leave this body and die at my hand. In the daylight, you will rot and change into the lifeless being you should be, for the next night, your first night as the undead, Eferhild will rise, and Eferhild shall bring this world to its knees" Saying these words, I pull up my sleeves, the white fabric hiding my scared past on my back, helping me with this task of making one of my own. Slicing my naturally sharp nails straight down two lines on my forearms, I feel pain as only my own hand can make. The same straight lines that were cut for me three hundred years ago, sends a shudder of pain rushing through my body. The last time I felt this pain was the one time I tried this before, the one person whose blood overwhelmed me so it got him killed. A humans pain, I thought I had left behind, the memory of my dead lover swimming in my skull.

Cutting Eferhild's arms next, she pushes them towards me, wanting this as much as I want it for her. Ready and powered by the sight of my blood, she moves to place her mouth into my forearms, her logic being that becoming a vampire would mean needing to drink. How humans come up with these fantasies of my kind and what we must do to each other. Stopping her before she makes this impossible to work, my words freeze her mid-way.

"No dear child, this is not the way it happens. All the stories you've heard were wrong. You will not taste any blood until the night of your first night. That blood will soak into your awaiting organs when it is time, giving you what you need to shift. Not now when it will soak away for no good use." Raising her head, I lock our forearms on top of each other, our cuts ripping apart to let our blood flow and mix. "If I taste your blood, even a drop this will not work. To become a vampire you cannot have been tasted by that night creature" Nodding her head as our bloods mix and our skin rips further, our scars becoming one.

Forming a barrier of protection, our mixing blood begins to give off heat, my own blood seeping into Eferhild's warm blood, boiling our bodies as her blood flows into me. Dying my white cloak red, my sleeves have slipped down over our arms, covering us from the pain that is about to shoot into Eferhild's body. Why I chose white as my cloak colour tonight I am not sure, but what I do know is, the scream about to come from Eferhild's lips will not be like any that this whore house has ever heard before.

Moving my body closer to hers, Eferhild lets her first cry free from her lips, her fighting force behind the scream is like someone breaking ice cubes over my head. Screaming for one reason and one reason only, the poison in my blood flows into her human frail body, creating a reaction many do not survive. Seeing the vein pumping nicely in her neck, her main artery running under her ear calls out to me, the next pain she is going to feel will be even worse. To make sure my blood pumps into her every vein, it is best to let her own escape. To boost her with my poison my fangs will rip at her body, cutting her neck and arms and body, making sure she fills with my blood and losses all of her own.

Screaming out, I paint this already red room redder, biting and ripping at her shoulders and neck. Healing as she is reborn, I know the damage will not be everlasting; the problem with my dead lover was that I was too afraid to hurt him. Eferhild, I know is strong and will make it through this. Her skin in-between my teeth, I rip, making sure not to let a drop of her blood enter my throat. If I do this ancient performance will be for nothing, for when the drop of my lover's blood got my bottom lip, I could not stop.

Tightening her grip on my forearms as I put her through non-imaginable pain, which even an obsidian knife couldn't give. The most powerful weapon I have and the key ingredient of this ritual, my fangs thrum from pleasure at causing this pain. Never shattering, my teeth and my body are so strong and durable, that I can be thrown off the highest bridge in the world and I will never break. There are a few ways to kill us vampires but brute force is the hardest way.

Biting out her throat as the last of her blood leaves her; I can see all the blue lines filling her body, my blood and poison filling her. Spitting her throat out onto the floor, the other chunks of her body I have bitten of her lie around us, my liking the blood red flooring coming into play. Wanting nothing more than to die, I see the light going out in her eyes, as her death finally takes hold. My blue power overflowing inside her, they aim for her eyes, the poison finding its escape into the world by the only living organ that is on twenty-four hour show.

Pushing her body away from me, she hits the floor hard, her cold dead weight sending a shocking thud through the room. The morning light touching the sky so far away that I only see grey clouds, I move to the windows and rip all the curtains off. Needing as much natural light in the room as I can get, the bay windows mean her poisoned body will get all the burning light it needs to rot enough for her undead rising tomorrow night.

Stroking her face with the back of my hand, I blow out the small candle on the window sill and move inside the closet to seek sleep myself. Needing the natural day light for Eferhild's transition to work for me, I will burn up in moments if I do not hide myself now. Snug as a bug in my blood soaked cloak, I wait to hear her sobs, as her new dead life fills her body.

Hours have passed though I cannot seem to sleep. Sleep like any creature is needed so I can absorb the feed, especially after the big feed I had.

Still silent outside, I know it is too early for Eferhild's body to react to the poison. Young and healthy, I know this time it will work. My ex lover's body rejected the transmission because his body was already poisoned. Poisoned with a human disease, one that was more powerful than my poison, my power, he was never fated to join me in this afterlife.

Never a fidgety vampire, I am always able to close my eyes and at once be asleep. Why this night alone I am not able to, I do not know. Maybe it is because of the gift I have just given or the greediness of my feed. My body needing more time to absorb the blood, I feel it slowly working even though I do not sleep. Not positive, I feel if I do not sleep, I will go mad. This tiny wardrobe not helping, I feel sharp enough for the plan ahead.

 Closing my eyes once more, I relax the hold on my body hoping if I shift in the right way I may drift off. Moving right, I lean into the big fluffy coats in here, cocooning myself like a human usually would.

Comfortable, I lean my head back, the fluffy coats stroking my hardened face like a lost love. Seeing a street, I am puzzled, where has this street come from. Night time, the street has identical houses running down either side, the cobbled ground empty of any items or people. Lights going out, I use my sharp vision to look at where the lights have begun to go out first, this odd place feeling cold and wet.

Grey, is all I can see. A grey cloud of some kind, thick and deeply rooting itself to the stone work around, it travels down the road, creeping its way towards me as if I am its target. Taking over everything before me, the cloud seeps into every crevice it can find. Stuck where I am, the cloud snakes closer like it is alive on its own, the fogginess seeming to sweep over my mind. Appearing as if a magician is performing to me, a pair of hands comes out of the substance, the hands actually being the same substance as the grey, they reach out to me. A breath away, the cloud is going to consume me, I can feel it, see it. Rising up to envelope me, the hands going for my face, a sob echoes in my ears.

 "Pain… so much…" Eferhild's voices breaks into my sleep. Never dreaming of something so vividly, my hands shake as I place them on the doors in front of me. Shaking uncontrollably, how is this happening. First I cannot sleep and next my body isn't in my control. So this must be what it feels like when a vampire makes another one.

Ignoring my weaknesses for now, I push the wardrobe doors open, Eferhild's sobs growing as her awareness comes back to her.

Lying where I left her, her body is still showing signs of the deep blue veins, still processing the poison through her system. Her brown eyes now a lighter shade than before; her pupils glow at me, the poison in her finding its way to look out at the world. Showing me that it has fully worked, her transformation will not be successful if her eyes did not look this way. Learning to hide this glow from humans is something she will have to practice, feeling the glow wanting to shine out is something you become aware of as your transformation becomes final.

Reaching down, I pull the girl the up, her sobs growing worse as I put her into a standing position.

"I know this hurts my child. However this is the only way, the only way I can gift you with your true life, your true power. Are you truly ready to begin this journey?"

Breaking the words she wants to say through her sobs she manages to agree. "Ye...Y... Yess" Sitting back, I flash the bed back into its original place so she can partly relax. "I want to begin." She hisses out through her teeth, her fangs on full display as she cannot yet hide them well.

Changing as quickly as I can, I throw on a new black suit, making sure to pack up all my other items of clothing into a small suitcase. Having nothing for Eferhild to wear, I slip out of our room and quickly look for the best outfit for her.

"Here put these on"

"Those are male clothes" She questions, confused as to why I am giving her a pristine suit I found two rooms down.

"These are male clothes because males have told you they are, now put them on."

"I like female clothes, I like wearing a dress and a corset" She huffs, her sobs completely gone now the half moon is fully in the sky on its own.

"Well for tonight, you wearing this makes it much easier for your first hunt. If you wish to wear a dress after tonight, you may"

"Maybe I will wear both trousers and dresses" She says, her own self-worth growing back into her as the power of her new body settles into itself.

"If you wish, now we must get going." Hurrying her to change, she ends up breaking a floor board beneath her when she steps into her trouser leg far too quickly. Her new strength not yet discovered, her strength will only grow as she ages, my strength being far superior to hers because of my age.

By the time she is ready and annoyed by the fact she cannot look in the mirror to see how she looks, the wardrobe door is hanging off, the bed has two broken legs and the chair in the corner has been smashed to pieces. Watching her wreck the place by accident is quite funny, her new body exhilarating her, as well as scaring her.

Calming her about the mirror, I inform her I will teach her when she is ready about looking into someone else's mind to see what she looks like. However it will not work on me, as I am older than her, my mind stronger than hers to penetrate.

"What will we do about the room?" She asks, her sharp eyesight, scanning everything she has damaged.

"I have paid in full. You should know better than anyone that there are no limits to what a client can do in a whore's room" I say raising an eyebrow.

"I cannot leave here like this, they will recognise me." She wines scolding my choice of fashion again. "I maybe in a suit, but I still look like me, still have my long blond hair, and female features."

"If you are on my arm, which you will be, no one will question us. I must hold onto your arm so you do not over step and flash quickly before everyone. Revealing our secret...that would make everyone turn on us."

"Flash. Is that what you call it when we move faster than sight or sound?"

"Yes" I say picking up the suitcase, ready to leave.

"You know people know of vampire's right. It's not a big secret like you think" Rolling her eyes at me, she pulls on the main door breaking the hinges slightly as she does.

"Eferhild, people may know of vampires in their minds but the truth of us would terrify them. You are special in the calmness you had in seeing truly what I am. In that I knew you could, would become one of us. Now we must be going, you cannot wait much longer to feed. Your food is waiting for us I'm sure." Smiling at her, I take her arm as we leave our room.

Exiting the whore house, I throw the room key to the barman, all the whores eyeing us as I take their upper class friend from their dirty world. Quizzing each other with looks as to why the old Claire gets to leave with me, I feel her pride that she is free from this place. Her power beyond the men she used to serve, the surprise I have planned for her will feel even more delicious when she finds out what it is.

$$\mathcal{V}$$

"Ashwood Street" Eferhild whispers, hoping the silent house will not hear us.

"Surprise" I say, tapping the bottom of her back to start walking again.

Leaving my suitcase and carriage a few streets away, my driver has also wondered off for a meal for the night. Making him wait a whole day for me to return to him on a regular basis, he knows to go find things to do until I return ready to move onto the next place.

Situated at the end of the long street, the Ashwood estate is a dark part of the city, the Ashwood Manor definitely not being a building anyone can miss. Revenge is the perfect first feed Eferhild can have, her appetite for death will not be an issue with these people. Her own need for this to happen as soon as it can we quickly make it to the front door, the fine detailing on the wood surprises me, the carvings depicting a strong warrior with slaves all around it. This is the home Eferhild was willing to call home.

Brushing off the kind of person she was to want to live in a place like this as the property of a man, I raise my eyebrow seeing her need to get inside already.

"You have a few options here"

"And what are they?" She asks, her hunger growing tenfold, since she still has not feed after a few hours of her change.

"Option one you can make it slow, being so careful that not one of them is expecting what is to come. Two, you can make it scary, putting fear into every food source before you eat and take what is yours or... your final option." Stroking the carving on the door, I feel her body go rigid next to me.

"You can make this a bloodbath."

Turning my head so I can gauge a reaction from my new protégé, I feel proud at the look I am receiving in return.

"If you are hungry enough Eferhild, which I know you are. You can knock on this door and make you way throughout the manor eating anything you can. Blood and terror will follow in your wake as you make it towards Clive and his new bride; the mess you make will forever be talked about. If you let your inner vampire free on this night, I promise I will teach you next time how to control, stalk and scare your prey. For this first time do not hold anything back"

Looking at me as she thinks, I see the beast in her begging to be set free by her face, her revenge fighting her over the need to just feed on whoever she can.

"How about this... you knock on the door and begin feeding. I will find your lovely ex fiancé and keep him and his wife waiting. Waiting for you, hearing the revenge you are havocking throughout their manor until..." I stop

"At last..."

"You make it to them?"

Not saying a word, Eferhild knocks hard on the door, her fist making a dent in the warriors head as her agreement to my last offer is made.

Opening cautiously, a finely dressed man in his late twenties looks out with confusion, wondering why someone would dare knock at this manor at this god foreskin hour. Before he can get a word out, Eferhild jumps onto him, her fangs darting straight to his throat, as his blood breaks his skin to the open air.

Clearly a very quick learner and a better student than I was, Eferhild keeps every drop of blood for herself, her need to drink everything in this man soaking into her mouth. Drinking him dry before he can even cry out, she darts off into her old home, knowing exactly where her next prey lies.

Stepping inside, I close the heavy oak door, the wind trapping inside causing a loud bang. Breaking out into the grand hallway, the oak wood décor is everywhere. Stained red, I laugh thinking how funny that they have already stained this house maroon, many generations before this one, showing the future bloodbath to come.

Walking straight ahead, I make my way through the manor, hearing to my delight the terror of the people finding themselves awakened by teeth entering their throats, arms or legs. Wondering if she is being as controlled at keeping every drop of blood in her mouth now that she has feed a few times, I slowly walk past one room where two heavy breathes can be heard. Knowing it is the owner of the house, Senior Ashwood and his wife struggle more with their deeper breathing, the long lives they have had showing their lung capacity.

Walking up the hall, I am taken to another set of stairs. Following it, I hear the cries of death getting closer, Eferhild making her way through the house in record time. Her need for revenge, for food is driving her faster through the house than a two hundred year old powerful vampire could even do.

Stepping off up the last step, I find myself at the end of a short corridor with one room waiting at the end. Wallpapered walls, the green looks like scales of a snake wanting me to wind my way to the door. Ferns potted on either side, I take hold of the door handle, the panicked breathes coming from inside clearly think I am the one who has come to hurt them.

Taking hold of the golden handle, I twist, hearing the subtle creak of the door, my own power of opening it so slowly it scares the people inside further. Bringing darkness down around me fully, I open the door wide to see two figures lying together huddled in a bed.

My own instincts and hunger jumping forward, I crave to eat myself. Knowing all they can see is black, I step into the room bringing the darkness with me. Squealing a little, the sound comes from the man not the woman, the weakness I can feel of his fear washing over me cries how pathetic he is. Bangs echoing down the waiting hall, their eyes grow wide as the sound of Ashwood's parent's murder screeches up the hallway to their son.

Moving to the woman's side of the bed, the candlelight here brightens up each side of their bed. Pushing my darkness onto the candle the flame goes out with a puff, my darkness holding down a trail of smoke that should be reaching up to the ceiling. Bringing Clive's wife into the night, I feel her hand shake so badly as she pulls her covers further over herself to try and find some protection from the screams. Screaming out himself in pure terror, the young Ashwood heir jumps out of bed and runs to the closest window.

"Do not leave me!" The wife cries, her fear locking her on the bed.

Opening the window, I see the walkway; build outside the window, connecting the roofing of the whole manor. Stepping one foot out of the opening, a creaking comes from the hallway making the two humans pause. The last candle in the room going out by my power, I feel the shiver run through both their bodies. Light now only coming from the moon shining in through Mr Ashwood's escape route.

"Clive darling... where are you off too?" Eferhild's elegant voice sings as she steps out of the darkness I have created, the full moonlight brightening her image in all the power she now has.

"Claire?" Clive Ashwood asks

Dripping with blood, Eferhild has more blood on her now then clothes. Taking of the suit jacket and trousers, I see they were clearly getting in her way when she hunted, her newly formed legs of muscle show a woman that no man would dare try to mess with.

With just a blood coloured shirt and tie left, Eferhild lets out an over excited laugh. Her excitement echoing into every fibre of the woman under my darkness, the bed growing cold under the sweat dripping off her every crevice. Her body shivering too, I feel the blood soaking inside my number two, the new power coming from her body now feeding greedily off the amount of blood she has consumed.

"So you recognised me?" Eferhild says, moving over to the bed as I step back letting my darkness let light seep only upon my protégé and her blood covered face.

"Amelia... how cold you look tonight. I can help with that..." Eferhild whispers, pulling on the covers covering Clive's wife, the woman having no fight in her letting it fall with my protégés over powering presence. "I can help you feel some warmth come back into your short lived life."

"Sh...short lived?" The woman on the bed stammers.

"Well of course. Your husband doesn't care if you live or die, as long as he can escape" I say from the corner letting the candles shoot back to life, the light in the room revealing myself to her. "He has fled after all"

Clocking the window where her husband once was, Amelia stammers as Eferhild climbs on top of her. "Feel the warmth I spoke of?"

"N... no. You are colder than me" She puffs the temperature in the room dropping from our over powering presence and darkness. Shivering beyond the point of being alive, Amelia's hair at the roots begins to turn white, her face growing into a shadow of pure terror. Looking to me, Eferhild looks as confused as I am, a grey wisp of smoke circling around Amelia's eyes, the smoke be so faint that if you were not my kind you would miss it.

"Amelia?" Stepping forward, I tell Eferhild to go after Clive. Her main revenge cannot be taken from her first feeding.

"Amelia? What is happening to you?" Sitting on the bed next to her, I hear the terrifying scream of Clive making its way back to my ears, my protégés revenge being fully complete as she takes her time to let him scream for her.

Stretching my hand out to the young woman, the coldness in the room has stayed, my presence not being the culprit.

Flashing grey, my mind goes blank; a sharp pain shoots through my skull as I once again see the hands outstretch, they come for me, the woman before me coming back into focus as the smoke around her eyes dart at me. Pushing myself back, I flash away from Amelia, whatever this grey substance is it still comes for me. Dodging too hard, I land firm because of the pounding in my head the floor becomes my friend, the grey wisp floating away over towards the green hallway. Amelia, frozen in place, her hair has become completely white; no such beat comes from her chest anymore.

"What happened to her?" Eferhild voice breaks my daze of grey clouds and Amelia's terror.

"I think we terrified her to death." I ponder, flashing to my feet as close as I can to the door.

"What is the matter Cayden?"

"I am not sure, but I need to find out. Find some clothes. Your revenge is over, we need to leave" Nodding to my command without question, Eferhild moves from the room, her own old dressing room being somewhere in this grand manor.

Three

"What of all the bodies and blood we are leaving behind?" Eferhild asks as I escort her casually down the front steps of the Ashwood estate.

"Usually I would clean up, hide any sign that something like the humans call murder has happened. For this case, I think we should leave it, make a statement to the city that even if you are one of the most powerful families that terrible things can still happen to you. From the way they treated you though Eferhild. It would surprise me if many other people are not happy this happened to them."

"So when we were at the whore house, who did you end up feeding on?"

"Two gentlemen and a whore they had a deal with."

"Oh you mean Sara." Eferhild states sounding a little unsure about hearing the death of someone she knew.

"Does it bother you that I killed her?"

"In fact..." She pauses, making me wonder if I may have hurt her now "No. It may seem bad but I don't feel sorry that I killed every single servant in the Ashwood home. Is that a vampire thing? Will I never feel anything again?"

"No you shall definitely feel again. When a vampire feeds, your natural instincts take over; in a way it is the part of you that is most human, most primal. Your need to feed, to eat is in every animal in existence. Take the Donna party for an example, you've heard of them yes?"

Shaking her head, we turn from the Ashwood Street, our brand new clothes hiding us in plain sight. If anyone looked at us right now they would only see two very regal citizens of the queen, causally on a midnight stroll. Feeding mainly on strollers, you would think many people wouldn't think of walking through a darkened, high built area where anything could be waiting, but for me, dinner always comes fairly easy.

"Oh of course, you have been out of high society for the last year or so. The Donna party were a family travelling to the new world, moving to start an even better life. Out of eighty-one people, families and solo travellers, only forty-five made it through a terrible harsh winter stuck in some mountains." I informed her like a teacher in a school.

"And what has this got to do with human instinct?"

"The only way the forty-five party members survived is because many of them had to eat the ones that died. The instinct you felt when feeding, what you feel now... or don't feel. It is a natural instinct of a vampire to be fine with killing humans, even innocent ones. We are the hunter, they are the prey." I state, taking her towards a local park I know in these parts.

"So this Donna party felt no remorse for the eating of friends and family members?"

"I do not know the answer to that question. I only heard the story when they came here to England, not first-hand knowledge. This does not matter. I just wanted to make my point."

"Does this mean I can never have a friendship with a human again? Will I only ever see them as food?"

"Did you only see lambs as food when you were human or did you think they were cute and want to save them when your father wanted to cook it?"

"I didn't live on a farm so my father would never be the one making that decision. He would tell the head butler what he wanted and it would come, though I see your point. Where are you taking me?"

"To one of the nicest parks in this area. I want to show you some of what you can do before I send you off alone to my estate. I am not sure how long my investigation in to the odd death of your ex-lovers wife and the flashes I keep getting will be."

"Odd flashes?" She asks, concern filling her voice.

"It is of no matter at this moment. You come first; after all, finding out about whom you have become Eferhild will be an exciting time for you. I do wish I was there to watch you go through it. It has been three hundred years since I first turned and to witness it again would make me smile. Seeing your natural talent at devouring the Ashwood home, I see you are going to learn very quickly indeed." Opening the squeaking metal gate, the bricked archway hides the natural world we are about to step into, a polar opposite from the city greyness behind us.

"First and most important, once you return to my estate and when you feed, clean up after yourself. And I mean clean. Make sure no trace can be found. I have made a perfect home for myself there and I do not want you ruining it. Every person or home in the local villages and the local ones I must tell you are pretty far from my home, they are off limits. Though if you let yourself get too hungry the doors with my sigil on it are the most protected, and I will show you my sigil when we return to the carriage. The driver is also off limits." I growl, turning to her before we walk into the park. Pulling even more darkness down around us, the moon in the sky vanishes as her eyes latch onto mine.

"He knows of what I am, in a kind of way and he is fine with it. His family has been driving me around for generations and I would like to keep it that way. You can ask for his services whenever you like. But if you harm him or his family I will not hesitate to kill you. Eferhild, as much as you amuse me now, his family was with me first and loyalty is everything to me." Nodding her head with one dip, she looks back at me, fear circling her new bright pupils.

"I understand, but when will I know when I'm getting too hungry? I do not wish to do something silly?"

"Feeding on the local animals in my forest will help you with the hunt and controlling your need, but it will not stop the hunger for long to feed properly. If you try only surviving on them, you will die. Do not wipe out my wildlife please; I am fond of nature's creatures filling my protected land. Feed and train yourself but go hunt properly when you need to." Motioning for her to step into the green land, I let the moon's glow shine down upon the only two figures in this vast park.

"How will I know when I am in a true need for feeding?" Eferhild quizzes, suddenly looking a little afraid of being left alone on my land.

Understanding her fear of learning all about becoming a night creature on her own, I feel sorrow thinking I should have been there helping. Helping her hone and discover every new talent she may possess. Even after three hundred years I know that I have only discovered half of what I could potentially do. Living a simple life of knowledge will do this to you. Holding out my arm once again, she locks hers through mine as we being to wander out into the fogginess covering the hills down into the park.

Definitely not hungry after the bloodbath and feeding she has just had, this is the perfect time for her to concentrate on the parts of her vampirism that will help her with her training. Walking like a married couple, as if it was a bright spring morning, I can still feel her body wanting to zip off as fast as it can.

"Would you first like to run? Let this energy building up inside you out or would you like to find out more?" Remembering the feeling of your body wanting to run itself in any which way it can, I know what her answer is going to be.

"I want to know of what more I can do" Surprising me, I dip my head in admiration.

"Lets us find a spot to sit"

Wondering, I let the world around us be, let it waken up to the sounds of nothingness. Being a night creature, we do have the talent of not making a noise if we don't want to. Unlike when I was walking to the Ashwood room, I purposely heaved my steps to pound fear into Eferhild's awaiting victims. Now we are like the wind, stepping onto the gravel sprinkled beneath us without actually touching it.

Every idea out there about our race is shrouded in wonder and untold truths. Figuring out the fact from fiction is even hard for me, as a lot of what I can do is pure instinct. No thinking or spells are needed to perform what I wish; my body helps my wishes come true. The fact that neither of us can be heard walking right now is solely because Eferhild's is using her instincts to hear the silence around us. The poison in her new body is making sure she doesn't make any noise, all so she cannot be spotted by any potential food or danger.

We make our way down the steep hill, from this view you get a clear sight of the city circling us. I never usually take note of which city I am in. The funny fact that always seems to happen is that I can see our country's flag flying high upon the cities palace, signalling the presence of Queen Victoria. No matter where I go, she seems to be there also, a royal stalker without actually knowing she's doing it. Whether it is because my carriage driver only likes to go where she is when I tell him to take me to a city, our red and blue colours stand out from the grey old buildings of this city.

Lights on here and there, only the main streets and richer parts of the city will have lamps lit, these parts of this city are usually much quieter. Loving the darkness, as much as night creatures do by our lives being only in the dark, the poorer citizens of this city, of any city let their own darkness out when the sun goes down.

Pointing out a collection of bright lights coming from a circle of building far in the distance I ask Eferhild is she knows what it is.

"That is circular lights of night. It is a place built purposely for traveling circuses and performers to stay and put on a show for the rich. Many families go, though I believe in the next few evenings, according to clients from the whore house that the queen is going to view a very special show done by a French group of performers" Sounding very void of emotion, I can still feel her resentment at the elite of this country, the people who let a man throw her out into the street as she is nothing.

"Have you ever been?"

"My father took me and my brother once when we were very little. Mother didn't approve of shows where woman did physical things like the trapeze." Letting go of my arm as we make it to a quaint bench under an ancient oak tree, Eferhild puts on a high shrivel voice. "It is not proper for women to wear tight clothing, and hang like a monkey from the air. Honestly how will women ever gain respect if they continue to flounce around in front of men in this ghastly way?"

Laughing at her voice, I place myself next to her, sitting so my arm slides along the back of the bench. Sitting back in her old clothing, Eferhild's back doesn't touch the bench but is straight up, looking as if she will jump to her feet in a moment if need be.

"Relax Eferhild. You do not need to be of high class when it is just us"

"It is not for you. I prefer sitting like this. Slouching for that year in the whore house has done my back in. I don't know how you men do it so much."

"For one, I am a night creature, so back pain isn't something we get. Yours will disappear as the poison in you settles your new body. Pain is something only the best of best can do to us. Of course sunlight is painful and so is fire, but pain isn't a feeling I have had to deal with much over the last three hundred years"

"How does it feel to be so old yet not age?" She asks the question I never had to chance to ask.

"In some ways it feels natural. After the point where you watch people age and die while their families carry on like my carriage driver and his family, you see that the need for children is not there. I do not age or die so children are not needed to grow and carry on my line and life. As everyone I knew when I was human have not existed in a long time and like you I did not see them before I became my true self, aging has never been a problem. I do not remember who I was or about my life as a human, but after three hundred years that is now a shame."

"If anything, aging and the growing of a population is pointless if everyone was able to be like us." I inform her of a fact I have begun to theories over the past few years.

"You do not remember your past? Willi forget mine?" Her question making me wonder if she would want to remember hers or not.

"Do not fear, I do not know why I do not remember my past but I know it is not a thing that happened because of my vampire status. Every other of our kind has full memories of their past.

"If everyone was like us though, wouldn't we die? You said yourself that we need human blood to live. So in theory, if everyone was a night creature like us, we would all eventually starve and die after killing the whole planet of wildlife hunting for some kind of food source. In the end if everyone was like us and tried to live forever in the night, the world's creatures would die and then nature could take back its hold of this blue planet." Eferhild counters my thoughts, taking away the idea of a new night world.

"So it couldn't happen. We cannot create a world for night. That is a shame" I say, wondering how I didn't see the logic in this myself. Distracted by the thought of a new world, I must have squashed the logic I would usually have over all others, my desire to win this world over my own evil kind clouding my judgement. "You have already trumped me as your teacher. I knew you were a great choice to change"

Moulding her mouth into a cheeky smile, her fangs pop out making me laugh again. The control she will have over her new body has not yet become hers yet.

"You could in theory turn a huge part of the population you think is worthy and use the rest as cattle. Just as humans do with animals they view themselves better as. Do we have to kill our prey to survive or is it a need we just want and feel?"

"You view yourself as better than them then. You are but a babe" I tell her, as her body lurches suddenly, the flash in her wanting to be used. "But your question is just, we do not have to kill, but it takes a lot of self-control not to keep going. Even I would struggle to stop feeding. I myself enjoy the moment a human's soul leaves their body through my own lips."

"I view you as better than them. I am but what you can make me. I can become better than any that you have turned before, of this fact I am certain." Flashing to her feet before I can say anything, she darts off into the fog, the white clouds creeping back into the area we are in.

Raising an eyebrow, I let my hearing fan out. Taking control, I use the senses I have to alert me to when she will come back. A scratching in the east, I block it out knowing it is a just an owl perching on a tree. To the he right of me the rustling of leaf signals a harsh gust of wind moving in, the tree branches creaking as the oak behind me does it's best to not let the wind break any of its arms.

Closing my eyes, I let the world into my hearing, smiling at having to work hard to hear her. It has been a long time since I last had to use my instincts on an enemy, even one so young and untrained. It is surprising what one can do when they set their minds to it.

Closer than I thought she would make it, I hear the rustle of Eferhild's dress as she flashes from behind the tree. Darting at me with her hand outstretched, I can see it in my mind's eye as I wait till the last moment to move. Feeling the connection we share as creator and protégé, my body tingles at her presence near me, it telling me the control I could easily have over her will. A centimetre from my shoulder, flash to the right straight into the spot she was only a few minutes before.

Unsure how to stop herself with her mind gripped onto getting me, she smashes through the wooden bench, denting the metal frame work as she lands face down in the gravel before me. On my feet as I felt the wood splitting, as she went through it, the old bench sits in ruins around us.

"My, what have we done here Eferhild" I scold her in a joking tone.

Growling like she did back at the Ashwood estate, Eferhild turns onto her bottom, her dress torn from the breaking wood. "How did you know I was there? I had you, I was so quiet, I could feel how quiet I was." Seeing in her what I felt when I was first turned, I let her down gently, telling her the truth how in two ways I knew she was there.

"I knew you were there because I heard your dress as you moved from the tree. Like I said when we went hunting to the Ashwood estate, a woman's dress will get in your way if you want to surprise your victim. Men's clothing is fitted and tailored to our bodies so not much noise comes from us. Though at the speed you were moving, any human would never hear you coming. Only a vampire of my age and pure concentration could hear you coming. For a night creature that only turned today, that is a feat." Helping her to her feet, I see the proudness in her tough set jaw. Sad to let her know the fact I am about to say, I wonder if it will change the way she is feeling about this new life of hers.

"The other way I knew you was there is, I could feel you. As my protégé I will always feel you near me, always have a feeling of you when you come close to me. In a way I might be able to control you, have you do my bidding." Looking hurt, she steps back from me, her new found freedom disappearing before her eyes. Not certain that the rumours of this feeling were true, I had thought the vampires I have seen under their master's control had just been showing pure loyalty, now I know this may not always be the case.

"Am I your slave then? Another girl to add to a master and his wants. You said this was to free me, make me something I should always have been. Create me into someone far stronger than any man can control... was it all a lie...master"

"I am no man-" Cutting me off, she spits at me.

"You are worse than a man. Chaining me to your forever, making so I do anything you want. You are worse than Clive Ashwood" Letting it happen, I feel her claw scrap across my cheek, her nails so hard they can now pierce my rock hard skin.

Stinging, I hold strong as my deep blue blood seeps out of me, five scratches covering my face from the hurt, my protégé is feeling. Shock filling her face now, I can see what a child she still is. Only wanting to impress me with her show of talent after the bloodbath, the information I have given her might break her. The only thing I can do now is hug her, cuddle the hurt, the distrust of me out of her.

Pulling her by the arm, I bring her into my strong hold. Locking her in my strength, I hold her into my love; love that as a vampire I have only felt a few times in my long life.

"Eferhild. You are the only person I have ever turned, the only person it has worked on. Once I tried it on a past love, a love that died. You, my Eferhild are my protégé, not my property or possession. I have no want to control you. The natural instinct in me that feels you near me is like all the gifts we possess, an instinct. Together I hope to discover what we can both become. What we both can do." Holding her out at arm's length, she seems like a broken girl, having had enough of men and their promises. "After three hundred years of this life, I have only discovered half of what I can do, can achieve. Once I have dealt with whatever is happening around me, with my dream and Ashwood's wife I shall return to you. Together we shall form our own reign of night. How does that sound?"

Reaching up to my face, she feels each individual scratch she has created, my skin already healing at an accelerated rate. "What dream?"

"While you turned, I dreamt of grey, of a cloud sweeping into our world. Reaching for me, it turned into some kind of hands, its need to have me shredded through all that I am. I could not sleep, which is odd for a vampire. Our coma sleeps come easier than our need to kill." Closing my eyes again, I see the image of the small wisp of smoke leaving Ashwood's wife, a new sensation I haven't felt in a long time caressing my hurt pride, the feeling of fear. "I then saw a flash of it and a wisp of smoke wanting to come for me from Ashwood's wife, I think it has something to do with her being petrified."

"You've never seen that happen before?" She asks moving from my embrace.

"No"

Picking up a piece of the broken bench, she flips it in her hand, her dress in tatters. Watching her juggle a piece of the bench, I know she will take a while to forgive me for the betrayal she believes I have committed against her, time will be its only healer.

"You said you have never turned anyone else before. Am I truly the first? Even after three hundred years" She asks, her mind clearly wondering from topic to topic.

"No never. My love-" Cutting me off again, she holds her hand up.

"Do you promise you will never use your will over me, to control me against my wishes? Unless I am doing something so against your views, do you promise to let me live my life and have my freedom?"

"I do. Eferhild. I turned you for the better of you. I turned you so you can be free from control. I do not wish to have this over you. I wish for you to be by my side, not under my foot."

"Your face?"

"Will heal"

"I am ready to go. I think I have had enough for one night."
Looking up at me, I see the spark that was there before I told
her of my hold on her. A hold that is faint. From what I can
feel, if I do not use it, it will grow weaker. As she grows in
strength, my hold will vanish to nothingness. The only part I
know I will forever have will be the ability to know when she
is near me.

"Let us go... just" Motioning at her outfits, she laughs at
herself.

"I look as if I have been attacked by a bench"

"Will I think you did the attacking but you are correct. You
cannot walk in the street looking like this. We must flash to
the carriage. Too many questions will be asked and with the
murders being discovered in the morning." Nodding at me,
she holds her hand out to me, my need to finish my sentence
not being there.

"Lead the way." She commands, her trust for me returning.

Four

With Eferhild on her way to my estate, I have a feeling it may be a while before I next see her. Depending on the outcome of this meeting, a journey may be ahead for me. It's been a while since I last made a journey of self-discovery, though many of my kind seemed to have them frequently throughout our long years. Laughing at myself for being giddy for it, I step out into the subtle lamp light.

Over the road under from me, an emerald door calls out to the rest of the street. Surrounded by grey dull bricks and pasty windows, this one house on the street has been looked after. Heavy patterned curtains hang closed, keeping the world outside away. The pompoms sewn into the lining of the fabric are like drops of mustard circling the open sign clipped to them.

The invitation opening up the house even to my kind, I stroll over the empty road. Knocking as it is only polite, I wait as silence reigns out from the wooden shield this house has upon it. No victim of mine waits inside, even on a hunting night; this is not a place I would look for prey. Waiting patiently, I feel a pair of eyes watching me from the right. Glancing there, two men of the lower life of this city walk past, eyeing me up for an easy target. Always on the hunt themselves, I can tell by the calmness in the first ones heartbeat, that his mind is sizing up if they can mug me before I even have a chance to scream.

Cities known for having rough citizens in them, it can't be helped that a man in a tailored suit on a street like this wouldn't stand out. My ginger locks and lust drawing status doesn't help me hide when I am under a door light.

Not wanting to have to terrify or even kill these two men quickly just so I do not scare of the fellow I am here to see, I knock again. Egging the second man on, I feel his adrenaline kick in slightly, my action making him think they have me sacred. Stretching my hearing into the door, I hope to see if I can get a hint of when the occupant will arrive.

Silence, like a death seeping into the heart of a young girl as she is taken from her parents into a pre-arranged marriage, I get nothing from inside the building. Feeling the heat of protection coming from the doorway now, I cannot believe I could think any different of the man inside. Of course magical wards would be up to stop my kind or any kinds from seeing what is in this building, for I came to him because I know he is the best and in being the best, one must first protect themselves.

An ancient ward of protection has been placed around this door, around this land. With this, I feel lucky I have chosen to do the polite thing and knock. If not, rushing into this building with its false welcoming sign could have gone a very different way.

Trying the handle as one last test, the metal object won't even budge. Turning it left, even with my supernatural strength does nothing. The family that live here have had a rich history, meaning the power imbued into this protection is not something to mess with.

Knocking one last time, I hit the door with three heavy lumps, throwing my muscles into every hit. If he won't come to politeness I think I should try what the two men planning my death would do... brute force.

Over my shoulder, I notice the two men have gone, either given up on me, or hoping to jump me when I leave this building. Taking that as I sign that the homeowner is going to open the door, I harden my movements, turning myself into a statue.

The door is flung open as a pair of dead black eyes stares out at me. Frozen themselves, the figure coming to life before me is of someone I have never met but heard a lot about.

Five 'ten, the man of African descent beams a tooth grin at me, the smile he has managed to keep even with the terrible water supply this city has to offer. Shaven hair, the man has cloths wrapping around his body, each layer a different shade of brilliant bright colours. Patterns that even match the curtains he must have hung up himself, the Shaman greets me well.

"Blessed my kin. An impatient one to find himself at my door on this dark night" His deep voice booms into my chest, his accent stronger now that it may have been when he was in Africa.

"Blessed Shaman" I nod, signalling for myself to be allowed entry.

"What is a fine old night creature doing at my door? Kill too many elite women, so you need me to find more to replace them? After all, many people will notice when they have not future brides to marry." He says in his accusing tone.

"Elite woman are not my chosen food source so no. I am here on other business. Private business" I insist, motioning once more for me to be allowed inside.

"My establishment has rules and if they are broken..."

"You shall snap your fingers and I will be so far out of here that I will be lucky that the sun doesn't burn me up?" I ask, raising one eyebrow.

Nodding at me, he beams me another smile, sending a thrill of the power he has through me. Unknown to me exactly, I am not sure what gifts a Shaman usually has. All I know is they can enter your mind, far better than any night creature can. For this reason I am here and that secret alone, I know I could never trust another night creature with the knowledge in my head. I do not plan on finding out what other things a Shaman can do, so irritating him is something I shall keep to a minimum.

Working alone stops the risk of someone else ruining the play I am making, but with a new protégé I may have to change this tactic. With Eferhild now my number two, it means once this is all sorted, I may have to teach her a thing or two about what not to do when meeting someone who has power we know nothing of.

Swiping his arm wide, the Shaman welcomes me into his home; the veil I feel holding me at bay from entering even with the door open, vanishes like it was never there. Walking in, shoes clicking on the wooden floor, I see that the panels have been painted red. Walls carpeted rather than on the floor, this world already feels upside down.

"Follow me night creature" He says warmly, leading me to a door under the stairs.

"My wife and child are up the stairs. My wife's gift has become too strong to bear being around me when I use mine. What it is to be a woman pregnant with your second child. Considering she didn't have any Shaman magic in her until she was excepting our first, her power has grown stronger with each passing day." Talking to me as if we have been friends for years, the Shaman walks down a bright yellow painted staircase, the depth of this basement being lower than any others in the city.

"I remember my father warning that something like this could happen. It is all fine of course. Once her powers regain some semblance of levelling off, it means she can teach our children far better than I can" Laughing at his own uselessness with his children, I know I must be giving him such a confused smile. What need does he have to tell me, a client, a stranger about his life.

"Forgive me" He says, moving us both into a heavy scented room filled with items of all different kinds and warmth that could smother a bear.

In the centre of the room a table with two cushions on either side of it wait for us, the furniture looking as if it has been waiting all my life for me. The pillow easily big enough for someone to fall asleep in, the Shaman take his seat immediately my cushion calling out to me to relax before I have even made my way it to it. Drawing me past it, a compass hanging on a brass chain from the left of the room, its perfect circle shape drawing me to touch it.

"I had a feeling you may need it for whatever reason you are here. Though depending on how this goes I might advise you not to take it."

"Why did you ask me to forgive you?" I say turning from the compass.

"I forgot that each time you come here, that you do not remember coming here. So I go on about Gloria and the kids and you look at me like I have just given you my heart in a single moment of meeting me" Confusing me more, I smile at the delusional man. What it must be like to have a memory that makes things up for you. I, as a night creature I have no worries about my memory, the poison that changed my life has left me with a brain that can soak up anything I want and have the ability to recall it all at any moment.

"Cayden McNigh, I know you find it hard to believe that your memory could be taken. But with the power my ancestors give to protect this home, it is hard to remember to take that curse away from you alone." Beaming at me again, the Shaman turns from me to mix us a drink from his personal bar behind him. Mini and cute, the bar is something only a non-alcoholic would drink from. The size of my bar on my estate does not need to be mentioned, especially to a man who clearly thinks we meet in his dreams. "Yes I know it is no way as big as the bar you have on your estate, however it does me fine." The Shaman comments, reading my mind so simply.

Wondering how he knows my name, let alone that I was just thinking that, I guess the questions I have about the Sharman's powers must be based on some sort of telepathy. Hands behind my back, I grasp the compass, and lift it marginally so the chain attached above me releases it into my hands.

Spinning like someone's possessed it; the compasses needles shift inside hard from one place to the other, making my hand vibrate from the need of it to tell me where to go. Is Shaman magic imbued into this compass as well, meaning it may not want to work for me properly.

"Scotch, hold on the ice and a single drop of blood." The Shaman impressed by himself at remembering a drink I do not remember ever telling him is my favourite.

"Thank you"

"So do you think you might want to try breaking the hold this home has on your mind when you leave this place? Or would you rather continue this little catch up every time?" Clearly bored himself from the fact that his clients can't remember a thing about their conversations he has with them, I wonder if he has other ancestor voodoo up his sleeve.

"I have come on other business, important business. I have lived on this earth for over three hundred years and I have never seen anything like this. Felt anything like this" I say moving to sit down in the puff of fabric provided for me.

"I have never seen you afraid before. It humanises you." The Sharman says, freaking me out once more.

"Thank you, that's just the kind of thing a night creature wants to hear."

"I apologise. What is this important business" Taking a swing of his own drink, I try to listen out for his heart though I am answered with yet again all a human would hear.

"I cannot sleep. Or rather I should say when I finally did I had the most vivid dream that felt if I hadn't woken up these fogged clouds would have got me."

"Clouds?"

"Yes a slow moving, reaching cloud of grey, seeping into every piece of this street I was on. Taking me for last, I do not know why, but it reached out to me, its powerful hands grabbing for my soul" I shudder, the memory feeling so real. I hate this feeling, this weakness of being scared. "How can I feel this way about a dream?" I ask not letting him answer. "That's not all though. I took my protégé on a hunt this evening."

"Very nice, do tell me of the death you have made tonight." He scoffs; giving me a look I know means he won't enjoy this part of the conversation.

"The last victim, or meant to be victim. Well she died."

"As do most when drunk by a vampire" He counters.

"Yes but this wasn't us. She was terrified, yes by us but this was another level, like something else was seeping into the room into her soul. Her hair started to turn white, the whole of her head, a sheet of a ghost. Not moving, it was like something came by and took her soul away with her. I have heard of human being petrified to death, but this felt like something more. Some divine intervention." I whisper the last worlds, knowing he doesn't believe in the divine but in the power of his ancestors and what they gift him with.

"Was there anything else in the room with you, anyone else when this happened?"

"No. I sent my protégé to hunt for her revenge when it happened." I smile remember the joy on her face at finally getting the Ashwood boy back for all he had done to her.

"Revenge, did he do something horrid to her in her human life?" The Sharman quizzes sitting up from the slouch he had become.

"Very much so, but this is not why I am here."

"No of course not" He agrees, the excitement at finding out what kind of man deserves someone to need revenge of them. "So if there was nothing else that happened, why do you think these two things are connected?"

"I saw a flash of the grey hands coming towards me when I tried to touch the girl. The same exact hands that came for me in my dream."

"Well that would connect them" He laughs holding up his hands to me. "If I could have your hands, we shall see if I can find out more."

Putting down my glass, the drop of liquid left flashes a brilliant gold as the candle next to us throws its light at the substance. Emptying my other hand into my pocket, I didn't realises I had been holding on to the compass this whole time. Uncertain if the compass is to be used for the issue I am having or for something else, I hope tracking whatever is after me, is going to be as easy as holding this compass up in the air.

Placing my hands gently into the Shaman's hands, my senses return mildly allowing me to feel the presence of power drumming through this man. Still unable to feel or hear his heart beat, the drumming coming from his core beating like the heat of the magical wards protecting the house I am in. The power flowing through him must be the power coming from his family ancestry, a power so old it could destroy everything in this world, I am sure of it.

Closing his eyes, he dips his head and beings to whisper words to himself. Deep in where he needs to go to gain access to his gifts, it gives me time to look at the wrinkles covering his hands. Not old at all, the man is probably in his early thirties, but his hands tell a different story. With his gift aimed through his hands, I guess the use of power damages the outer skin over time. Mumbling faster, I catch the end of one word, which is fully in an African dialect, his cracked skin hands crying out for a rest from the magic inside him.

His right hand twitching, my eye sees a glint of something in the corner, right behind the Shaman. A sphere of some kind, the object calls to me. Nothing on it or around it, the sphere looks to float like a ball of pale light. Glowing brighter as this man chants his family's power into the need he has of it, I feel his body go rigid as I am pulled from this world.

Darkness, I can no longer feel my body, can no longer feel anything. Not into my mind, I feel as I have been taken into a dark room, left here to wait until I am once again called upon.

$\mathcal{V}$

Dragged back into reality, I am no longer on the chair I was once on. Turning to calmness, the darkness I was in became a sanctuary as time stretched on, my own freedom from the hellhole humans are making of this world. Back in the overly heated room, it feels heavier than it did before, like the walls themselves are pushing in around me.

"You must leave night creature" The Shaman's voice calls down to me from a height.

Looking up to where his voice has come from, I see he stands at the top of the yellow staircase, a look of utter terror ripping across his face.

"What did you see?"

"Greyness, madness. Coming for you but not you alone. Anyone near you, anyone trying to help you will be caught up in it" His voice shakes as he says each word. The panic coming off him hits me in waves of terror, the feeling of knowing what he does scaring me too.

"I know the greyness, but what is it?" Flashing to my feet, I can move as freely as I could outside now, my power flowing back to me in full. Darting to the sphere far quicker than the Shaman's mind will be able to understand, I take it before the man before me can notice. "Why can I move freely in this home now? I can now hear your heartbeat" I tell him, this not scaring him in the slightest.

"The power my home had over you has been lifted. The curse following you has broken the power my ancestors had over your body and mind. You are free to come and go from this place and you shall remember everything. You are no threat to me… but the greyness." Moving to flee further into his house, I flash up the stairs next to him.

"How do you know I am no threat to you?" I shuffle forward so he has to step back against a wall.

"You told me once, even though you will not recall it. I know for truth that it is true, I feel it through my ancestors. It is why their power over you has been lifted. But please leave my home." He asks as politely as he can through the shuddering of his quick breathe.

"What happened to the woman in the house, can you tell me anything" I beg, needed something to go on.

"The woman died of terror, of the greyness touching her. It was protecting her from you, from your kind when it did what it did to her. The only way to stop you sucking her dry was to petrify her to death. Everything she was feeling when your protégé Eferhild was goading her was made tenfold by this greyness by its presence. It is hunting you, hunting night creatures" Shoving me to the door, the Shaman cries for me to leave, to never return unless this evil can be dealt with.

Giving me a goodbye warning first, his words scrape down my back like every swipe I have been inflicted to before.

"I tell you to run, to flee from this evil coming for you. You will not win, you cannot win. This power is too great, too raw to fight... the terror and pain will get what it wants. It always does."

Slamming his door in my face, I feel the emptiness of the street behind me. The laughter of the two men, who have been waiting outside for me this whole time, shakes into my ears like a song of a small boy calling out to someone for food. To the right, I see the first signs of daylight coming, my need to find a place to hide until the sun goes down, out weighing my fear of this greyness.

Whatever this evil is, whatever the Shaman thinks he has warned me against. He's wrong.

With no time to spare or fool around, I flash to the two guys grabbing one by the neck. Not stopping with my fast movement, I take the scared man beneath my grip to the nearest alleyway. Laughing no more, I dig in my nails, feeding off the way his eyes have become bloodshot. Fear pounding through him, I feed off it, his heart hammering at a speed far faster than anyone could even hope to do with a hammer. His lungs failing him with my tight vice on his throat, I give out a dirty laugh myself, loving how the tables have turned.

My own fear of something hunting me, a fear I haven't truly felt since the night I became a night creature, I let my strength take over. My anger bursting free I crush his neck, letting everything I feel out as it caves in completely, blood spurting all over the alleyway. The man's eyes rolling back from the excruciating pain I have put him through in a matter of seconds, I hear his heart giving out on him, his own body putting him out of his misery.

Delving in, I drink deeply, letting every drop tickle my mouth as it touches my skin. Filling me with fulfilment and joy, a calmness soaks into me, the fear of whatever I am about to go on the hunt for vanishes, even if only slightly and for a little while.

Letting the carcass of my fear and anger drop, I turn and sort out my coat. His friend clearly wondering what has become of us, I slowly exit the alleyway, wiping the blood I know I must have on my face, off. Brushing my hair back, I see his friend; looking the other way trying to decipher what could have possibly have happened to his dirty friend. The sun now about to break the skyline, I flash behind him, breathing a breath I do not usually have, onto his overgrown neck hair.

Not one to look after him, I can smell the dirt coming off him, the blood pounding around his arteries being the only alluring thing about him. A cheap farmers hat on, this man's face his looking away from me, his mind clearly high on something.

"Your friend is gone" I whisper into his ear, flashing away to the left as his spins around.

"You're all that's left for tonight" I flash past slicing my index nail quickly down behind his ear, my nail not piecing the skin but instead taking sweat off him.

Tasting it, I close my eyes from the thrill I feel as it enters my body, the salty type of sweat this man has actually tasting the best. Far better than what his friend even had for blood, some humans just have better bodily fluids than others, all thanks to a bloodline he probably knows nothing about.

"Who are you?" He shouts, panic pounding in his mind. Usually I would like to toy with ones like him longer but with my need of finding a place to stay quickly, I speed things up.

"What is your name?" I ask, stepping out of the shadows I have created around myself, throwing my eyesight so he gets trapped in it.

"Mmm... my name?" He questions, seeing my eyes for the first time, the pupils blowing his petty brain.

"Yes" I whisper sending the words so they caress his ears.

Turning to leave, I step forward again, taking his forearm. Looking deep into his eyes, I push my presence on him. Doing something I shall never do to Eferhild, I mask this creature under my command. Just like I had done to the barman two nights ago, I look deep into his dark brown eyes, sinking into his thoughts.

Seeing a rundown squat of a house, every part of it looks like it is falling apart. Moving inside and through his mind, I see the interior doesn't match the drapes, clean and stylized; he must live this way to prevent people coming close to his home. Sounding my voice in his mind, I pound into his head "Take me to your home"

Over and over again, I leave his head to see the world around us, my body starting to react to the rising sun. Saying the phrase aloud, the man jumps to alert, pulling me away from the sunrise by the hand. Eagar and frightened by my presence inside and out of his world, he rushes home like never before.

Five

Sleeping for a vampire is usually very easy, especially after a feeding. I am undead so it is more of a coma, I drop my eyes and my mind vanishes from this world. But now, I cannot sleep. Even tucked in this beautiful four poster bed with cream fabric everywhere, sleep eludes me. How the man who lived here can hide this from the outside world I am not sure, but the money it would take to decorate this place must be coming from somewhere.

Feeling as if I am a human, restless because I took a nap early in the day, the sun cannot penetrate this room, the curtains being so heavy they block every inch of the outside world away. Protected and cocooned in this house made for a king, my sleeplessness is driving me mad. The fear for the grey cloud is circling my mind but my issue is sleep, the dreams be dammed.

Closing my eyes again, I try and force sleep to happen, to make my mind relax like I did in the wardrobe. Taking air in and out of my lungs like I would as a human, I wait for something to happen, anything to happen.

My ears twinging, the deep breathes of the owner of this house sound next to me, his house being so small that the only other place for him to lie is on the lounge under the window. Contemplating eating him for something to do, I feel the edge of my mind holding back, knowing what I will dream if I fully succumb to my coma.

The grey cloud seeping around my soul, I feel it reaching for me even now. The Shaman was meant to help me but instead he has dragged my mind into a world of panic. Telling me to forget the evil and flee. How will that help me, eventually it will find me. Of course it will, with the power of terrifying a prey my protégé was going to kill, it must be able to find me anywhere; its power must be limitless.

Flashing from the bed, I move to my coat, searching for what I need. Two items, the first is the golden compass, looking as if it has been made by a magician from the detail engraved on it. Opening it up, it has six hands upon it, each meaning to represent something. The Sharman said it was for me to have, but not for finding the evil chasing me. If not, what can all these needles mean, each one must represent something.

Three of the needles point in the same direction, off to the east, the metal a shade of deep blue aiming out the window where the dirty man lies. One of the needles points north, bobbing back and forth as though something is on the move, the colour being a pale shade of red. The longest needle out of all of them the fourth, its sharp shiny point pinned directly at me. Standing out from the rest, this needle isn't made of metal but instead it looks to be made out of ruby. The final one and most intriguing is a simple looking needle, far shorter than all the rest it turns within the complicated workings of the machinery drawing my eye. Spins constantly, the grey needle turns and turns and turns seeming to be searching after something that cannot be found.

All clipped together in the centre by a golden pin, I close the lid, certain I will have to wait to find out what its main goal is for.

Pulling out of my pocket next, I feel the warmth the sphere gives off, the power ebbing from its tiny form calling out to anything around it. Glowing no more, I can't help but wonder how this thing is going to help me. Out of everything in the Sharman's home, this is the item that told me to take it, showed me that it was needed. Now if I only had magic on my side, I could activate this thing and find what I'm looking for.

Throwing the sphere from hand to hand, its smooth shell feels as though it could break in a second. The power coming off of it also hinders it to a delicate state, one wrong move and the item will be lost forever. The edges already look cracked, but what if I drop it or even knock into something with it in my pocket. What might be released, for something must lie within this thing for so much power to consume the darkness I present.

Stopping my movement, I place the sphere back in my coat pocket and move to my trousers. Pulling them back on, I am like any man and prefer to sleep in the buff. Even though I go into a coma, sleeping in clothes just is not comfortable, the passed out male on the lounge can assert to that.

Leaving his bedroom, I wander in to his hall, listening carefully to every creek my feet make. Wanting to hear how it sounds to walk like a human around his home, I let my weight shuffle me forward, the damp feeling you get of this house from the outside does not make it to the inside walls. Rubbing my hand down the corridor, I stumble past a room I must have dashed past when we first arrived. A library and a small one at that, I know it is more of an office but with the amount of books covering the wall it certainly feels like a library. One so quaint and private, anyone visiting might miss it entirely.

A desk in the centre, it is made of a deep heavy set wood, glossed so the mahogany finish matches the room, the legs are so thick that the desk becomes one plank of wood. A green shade covers the small desk lamp, bringing a perfect amount of light onto the desk. The only light in the room, the light is fixed so the reader can see only the book he is reading.

With every wall covered in shelving, I have a feeling a window is somewhere behind the built in structures, only from the outside the look of wood covering a broken window will add to this peculiar man's secret sanctuary.

Books on many things, he has categorised it by subject, his organisation skills clearly very prominent. Books on health and the biology of animals first, a whole bookcase is filled with the study of dissection, both animal and human. The next bookcase is filled with the study of psychology; a subject I know is hidden from most of the world. These books, pressed to perfection, are pieces of study the world has not yet found out about. How is this man, the one I thought stupid and poor, able to have all of these bindings. These are black market secrets even I would find hard getting my hands on here.

Picking out the first one on this shelf, I flick through it quickly taking in all I can from it in a matter of seconds. To take in psychology in its raw undiscovered, unpublished in the real world form, is hard to understand everything before me. Not made into an art where many people are using it and discovering new things every day, I only take some of what it says to heart. Already, only reading the first book, I see faults in the young doctor who is studying this field.

Placing the book behind me on the desk I move to see what other subjects this stranger I have made bring me to his house has. Chemistry, physics, everything in this room is filled with the nature of science and law. The bookcase before me now, is filled head to toe with books on the law. He even has books on the best laws to get away with, and defending yourself in a court proceeding, even a corrupt court. Sparking my interest for the pursuit of knowledge, I flash through a few of the books, making a nice pile over his desk.

Moving to the other side of the room, I am taken off in a new direction for this man. First is a small shelf full of fiction workings. Next are Greek mythology and vampire stories, making it a shame that the truth is, he is now mine, this clearly bright stranger doesn't know he has been taken over by a night creature he has stories on.

Underneath, is history books, dating as far back as they possibly can with our knowledge. Sections on pagans and witches, I wonder how his science connects to the gift these people are known to possess. I for a fact know they do, the amount of British citizens who have untapped power waiting at their fingertips, the shame of the Church of England ruining this once powerful people.

The last and most intriguing bookcase is one full of vampire books. Not fiction makings but these look to be of fact. The books spines reading, Dissection of a Night Beast by Aleixa Mantangus, meaning it was alive when it was done, for my kind turn to dust when we are killed. A Vampires True Lifespan by Lucas Dashwood, Vampires One O One by Victor Fran, and the list goes on. Where theses come from I have no idea, how they are even real is another matter.

These authors, I can't help but wonder who they are and how they know this information. Are they vampires themselves or men brave enough and clever enough to fool a night creature into telling them our secrets. Reaching out to a book called Other Forms by Aliza Chentas, I wonder if I can funnily enough, find out more about my own powers, maybe these are the books I have been missing for the last three hundred years.

Burning as hot as fire, I take my hand back, my fingers not even making it to the books spin before my hand started to burn. Looking to my fingers, the tips are singed black, the pain of what I actually felt still drumming up my arm. How have I felt more pain in the last few nights, than I have in my whole lifetime. What is happening in this world that my time seems to be coming to an end. Is it this evil, this cloud reaching for me, or is the universe done with my story.

"They are spellbound" The hard voice, sounding nothing like the panicked one I heard on the street, speaks from behind me.

Making me jump, me a vampire, I spin so I am on the other side of the desk away from the doorway. Standing there in just a pair of pants and a shirt is the man I made bring me here. Though not him exactly, his voice is lower and much braver, his whole transformed into a being of someone far superior.

Cleaned up and not a hair out of place, I see he must have cleaned up in his room while I looked around. His beard no longer everywhere, he has shaped it just as mine gets done by professional barber. His light ashy hair, which I never noticed was a lovely length, is slicked back over his head so it stays where he wants it to. Groomed to perfection, I can see the neck hair that crept up over his top in the street has gone too, this man before me being an entirely different specimen to the one outside.

Giving me a cheeky smile, the teeth I thought because he was poor where all rigged and yellow are oddly perfect now, pearling white as they shine at me. Clearly no longer under my control, his eyes are no longer glazed over but alive, taking my muscled upper body in. The one real thing about becoming a vampire is that your body does change to the perfection the Greeks thought their gods looked like. My body is something I was never ashamed of, but having this definition in my muscles, definitely isn't a bad thing.

Looking to his legs, I see a very well-muscled pair, his black socks hugging his carves so tightly I think they might break apart. Clearly going to the Rugby school where not long ago the game of rugby was invented, I give in and return his smile with a stern look.

"How have you broken from my control?"

"I was never under your control… though it was fun pretending to be." He laughs stepping fully into the room.

"That is not possible. I felt you bend to my will, it has never gone wrong. I saw it in your eyes, felt it in your mind" Moving over to his spellbound books as he calls them, he reaches for the one I was originally going for.

"A very good illusion spell goes a long way. It's a shame you had to kill my partner but these things happen." He comments like I only squished a fly and not his companion.

"You knew who I was all along?"

"No not at all. It wasn't until you came at us, used your speed and took my friend off, that I knew. I wasn't laughing at you by the way. It was all my friends doing. I had to play the part" Flicking through his book, his deep voice drums into my ears as if he is weaving a spell even now.

"What were you laughing at? What is with this pretend life of yours?" I ask, my curiosity overshadowing the fact that my control didn't work on him.

"My now dead friend" Turning so his eye lock into mine like it did to him only a few hours ago. "He's dead correct?" Nodding my head with a single dip he carries on. "Well my dead friend said how he would like to rob you; his hate for the upper class was tenfold. The fact that you ended his life in such a way and so quickly, would have angered him even more about how the upper class treat the poor" Laughing at his friend demise, I puzzle how close they could have really been with the coldness he uses when speaking about him.

"And your covered up life style?"

"Well that's ended with now. You killed my way in so I guess you will have to do"

"Me?" I ask confused to what he needs me for. Pulling the light of the room down over me, I show him that I will not be easy to kill, even with his magic.

"Calm yourself night creature, I do not wish to kill you. My dead friend was my way into the underground vampire population. I know he was being regularly fed upon by several different vampires from the look of the teeth marks." Twiddling his fingers like he is going to start up a spell, I tense my body as he reaches for another vampire book on the shelf.

"Vampires only leave two teeth marks if they keep it clean and wish for the food to return on a regular basis. How can you tell they were all from different vampires?" I say letting the light back into the room. No longer holding a book he has moved right up to the other side of the table.

"Every tooth, no matter the creature, changes between every specimen. Even in vampires your teeth are all different. Your teeth may have changed when they come from the poison entering your system but they are still your teeth. A distinction between width and size overall of your fangs, will be partly different with every vampire."

"And why is this so important to you?" I quiz

"Only a Vampire could ask a question like that?"

Turning from me, the man leaves the room in a slow stroll. Following him, I see he is returning to his bedroom, leaving my question to hang in the warm air like wet laundry.

Following him, I enter the room to find him in the bed, his covers pulled up snug around himself.

"Will you not answer my question?"

"Come back into the bed and I shall help you sleep. In night fall I will answer your question. Truly, I promise. With your sleep deprivation, I wish not now to answer. It will be easier once your mind is clearer and your body has soaked up my dead friend's blood fully."

Unbeknownst to him, my body has much more blood to soak up first. The three people I fed on the other night have still given me enough blood to last for a few weeks at least. His now not so friend, being my last quick meal will not be a soaked up for quite some time.

Taking my trousers back off, I climb back into the bed laughing at him, my nakedness not bothering the man.

"Why do you laugh?"

"I cannot sleep, what do you think you can do to help me with that?"

"I am a pagan, this is what I do." Leaning out of the bed to the left, he grabs something of his side table. Whispering a word so quickly I miss is, I know it is magic by the fact I missed it. As a vampire that rarely happens, my hearing being one of my best abilities I have on call. His power working quickly, the end of the item in his had begins to burn and smoke. Bringing it towards me, I sink lower in the bed, my body being very flammable.

"Do not panic. The fire only started the sage. The smoke is slow burning which will not affect your skin. Trust me."

Waving the sage around the bed, I breathe in the smoke, just like a human would again, my body automatically calming as I suck the herb in.

"Sage is the most protective and calming herb of all time. Do not listen to what is written in books or what a witch will tell you. Sage is the herb grown and moulded into the natural world to calm all evil coming at you." The pagan's words soothe my mind, his voice tickling itself over my hard skin.

"I am evil though" I let out, my body crawling further down into the bed covers so I will sleep.

"A night creature is not evil or good. No one is. Every person on this mother earth is neither. Each action they choose to take defines who they are, but we are all changeable. You hunt and kill to live, so do humans. You take joy in the fear you pound into people minds, and so can animals. Creatures, all of us, are here to live and sage is here to protect us from the evil someone is trying to attack us with."

Standing up out of the bed, the now stunningly naked man next to me, ties the sage so it hangs above us on the posts, the substance seeping its protective bubble to keep us calm and serene. Hunching back under the warm covers with me, I feel like a little boy having a sleep over with a best friend. Laughing at myself and this stranger, I remember I still do not know his name.

"What is your name pagan?"

"Why not stick with that for now?" He jests

Raising an eyebrow to him, I feel my mind clearing; the fear of the grey cloud dissolves in my heart as sage covers me in its light. Its caring feature changing me back to the hunter I was before the first dream I had. How can a dream scare one so much, I am not sure. Though a flash of the petrified girl's hair fills my mind, the sage's new protection working so fast it pushes away anything put inside my thoughts.

The pagan's hand taking mine, like he did in the street, my glazed over eyes find him again.

"These nightmares you have, the sage can always protect you. Nature is magic in itself and if you'll only be brave enough to trust it, it can do many things for you indeed. Forget your fears for today and wash away the demons coming at you. The sage shall calm you, and I, the pagan am here to heal" Letting go of my hand, I shuffle onto my side, the man next to me feeling like his is the one who has been around for over three hundred years.

After all I know, all I have experienced, how do I feel like the young naive one in this situation. Enveloping me in one of his strong arms, I hear the slow steady beat of his heart, his lungs breathing in the sage relaxing everything about him. Doing as I feel happening inside this human, I take in a deep breath, sucking in as much of the sage's power as I can. Sleep calling out to me, telling me to find it, hunt it and use it, I close my eyes, the pagan's last words shooting into my mind as my coma takes my soul away from this world.

"My name is Amara Aldwin... it means death protector"

Six

"It's night time" Amara's voice calls to my deepened mind.

Waking easily, I feel refreshed and alive, which is impossible with the fact I am undead. The sage clearly doing an amazing job at helping protect me from the grey cloud, a shadow moves over my vision.

Circling my coat as he looks in its pockets, Amara is fully suited, his attire going with the real him. How I didn't see the hidden truth behind his illusion when I went into his mind to find his home, his pagan power must be such a raw form of magic my vampire gifts are no match. What his power consists of against the power of a Shaman or a witch I do not know, all I know is he must be powerful to have been able to fool me, even to the point where he pretended to sleep when I told him to.

"Looking for anything in particular?" I nod at his hand deep in my pocket. "Protecting me some more?"

"I am not your protector. A protector is something you clearly do not need, at least that is what I get from the way to took out my dead friend last night. My name means death protector; I protect the dead in a way, not the undead."

"Now you hurt my feelings. That's not very hospitable of you" I pretend a frown. Flashing up from the bed, I speed next to the pagan, pulling his hand out of my coat to see what he is doing. "I have private items in here."

Grasped in his hand is fresh sage, its new scent flushing up my nose. Greyish leaves cover the small stem helping the purple flowers to stand out. "More protection for the undead that you do not protect?" I ask giving him one of the cheeky smiles he keeps sending my way.

"I am only being a friend looking out for you. It can't do you any harm to have protection against the evil coming for you. I can feel it a mile away, searching out the city. How you've made it this far I do not know but I will try to help you dead man" Nudging me, so I let go of his hand, he places the sage back inside the black pocket.

"Dead man is not something you call a night creature. Though if it means you are my protector, you can call me anything you want" Outright flirting with him, he laughs at me, before pinching my bare nipple.

"I have hung out some fresh clothing that should fit you. If you change and come meet me in the dining room, we can discuss the questions you asked me today. Not that I don't like looking at you naked, but I feel this conversation should be a tad more formal"

Pointing to the open wardrobe door, Amara gives me one last once over and then leaves. Plain yet elegant, the clothing Amara had picked out for me fits this style of this house well. Pinstriped, the navy suit has a tailored waistcoat and even a brass pocket watch. A complex carved pattern on the top represents something, my night getting better already with new shiny toys. Assuming its pagan, I suit up, even putting on the mustard silver tie Amara has laid out for me.

Not even glancing in the mirror, as after a few hundred years you get use to not seeing your reflection, I check my coat pocket for my stolen items. Always a thief, when you first start out as a vampire on your own, no money, no belongings, stealing is how you create the life you need.

Stolen from me, the items are not here, my pockets only being full of the sage plant. Grumbling to myself, I make my way down the hallway, using my hearing to find the correct way to the dining room.

Bigger than I first thought, the dining room is in the basement of the building, taking up the whole space so Amara can make a show of flare he has for entertaining. Light and airy, the room has panelling on every wall, the wood having been painted a bright white colour with light blue edgings. Taking the style from the French, the room is fresh looking; making this area a little sanctuary for Amara from the fake interior of the building I am in.

"Is the front of this building an illusion because when I think about it now, the rest of the street is very fancy" Moving around an intimate table filling the centre spare of the room, I lightly touch the top of one of the chairs, the wood feeling so new under my hand.

Placed on the table are my two missing objects, shining out from the white fabric draping over the tables sides. Set for two, the table has plates ready for a three course meal and wine glasses ready to drink any wine you could think of. Gaining a whiff meat cooking, I can imagine how my tummy would rumble at the smell if I was human.

"I do not eat human food" I tell him, moving to the sit in the chair Amara is standing behind like an awaiting waiter.

"I know..." He chuckles at my statement. Leaning to speak into my ear and I get comfortable, his voice caresses down my spine "Alas I am human so I'm afraid I need to eat" Pushing his weight away from my chair, Amara vanishes upstairs.

Leaning over the table I go to move my items, claiming them back as my prizes. Why he felt the need to take them and bring them here I do not know. All I know is these items are mine, and mine to use for this uncertain future.

His footsteps returning very quickly, he tuts at me before my hand can touch the compass. Wishing I had now gone for the bigger item, the sphere seems to question me for not taking it. Two very different things, I am not sure how they are going to help me get to where I need to be. What even does a glowing sphere do, calling out to e for what reason. Maybe one the pagan will have an idea about.

"Why did you steal my items?"

"I haven't stolen them. If I stole them you would never have seen them again. I brought them here as a sign that we shall get to the evil hunting you. Firstly though, food" Placing a bowl in front of me, I smile, as a bowl looking very much like blood soup becomes my starter. Placing a bowl of light green soup on his placement, I see what he has planned.

"Everything for you is animal blood. I haven't had time to go fetch a human and drain them of all blood" Amara jokes at me. "Vampires can consume blood from any creature correct?"

Seeming to ask me in a way that he wants to tick off information he isn't quite sure is true about my kind, I beam at him.

"Where did you hear this news? I only consume human blood. Your arm will suffice." Squinting his small eyes at me, I pick up my soup spoon and take a slurp of the warm blood soup.

Boiling and fresh the warmth of the blood as it fills my mouth is to die for. Never thinking myself to have blood cooked and warmed for a nice dinner setting, I now add another thing to my list of what this young pagan has taught me already.

"This soup is beautiful" I comment, giving my thanks to the chef.

"I have added a few things to it to give the blood more flavour as it isn't coming fresh from the body of the animal"

"It is lovely; I never thought to have blood prepared in this way. That may be because the hunt is one of the best parts of the feeding process, but it's something to think out for the future." I laugh, drinking down my soup quickly.

"Naturally." He nods, not phased by my honesty at loving the hunt of humans and their blood "Would you care for a glass of wine or blood?"

"Wine will do just fine." I say holding out my glass to him. Reaching for the closest bottle to himself, I correct him before he grabs the wrong one. "Has to be red"

His hand freezing, he moves it to the right and quickly fills my glass with one of the finest looking bottles of wine I have seen in recent years. Where does this pagan gets all his finery and money, I am certainly curious to find out.

"How does a pagan come into this kind of lifestyle and money? Are you a bank robber?"

Chuckling his hearty crackle of a voice, it takes him a few moments to get himself under control to answer. "Certainly not. I was a lawyer. That's how I made my fortune. Dropping back in to that line of work for only big cases, I have managed to find myself a life well enough to keep connections where I need them. My private book collection comes from the connections I have made defending the worst."

"So tell me, why is my kind of so much interest to you. I feel your power, I see no reason we could be of any benefit to you"

"It starts with my interests in general. I am a scholar in truth, finding knowledge and absorbing it is all I need to survive. Over the years and with my age growing, my own heritage and birth right has fascinated me more than anything else. Unlike my weak siblings, and forgettable parents, I have found out I am very adept at my gifts."

"And a pagan's gifts are what exactly? I haven't heard of a true pagan in many a moon. Not with all the Christians running around."

"My gifts are not important now; all you need to know is a pagan is nothing without his knowledge and mine will fade."

"Fade?"

"Both my parents have lost their minds, with age came mindlessness. Dementia. Early onset, both parents and my eldest sister have gone from our world mentally. I am genetically programmed to follow the same route and even after everything I have researched or studied, I will end up the same." Looking afraid of his own future, I do feel for a day creature that will eventually end up aging and leaving this world. Their simple bodies and minds have never been able to sustain the kind of information I or Amara are filled with.

"So you will lose your gift as you lose your memories. This is tragic but unfortunately a fact of human like and even one such powerful pagan as yourself will have to live with."

"Unless, I do live but never age"

"Oh I see… Amara" Putting his hand up to me, I stop my words letting him have his say before I shut him down for good.

"I know what you are thinking. Why would you turn me, a pagan? What does doing that entail but I tell you now, you turn me and it could be the best thing that happens to you"

"Me?" I ask my voice jumping a little as to how that can work.

"Yes you" Taking a long drink of his wine, he finishes his glass, my hearing picking up the increasing beat of his heart, the blood pounding up his neck begging me to take a bite. Lucky for this pagan I am full and he is already feeding me more blood, stopping my natural instinct to dart at him. "I am a pagan and I am one of the only ones powerful enough to help you with this sphere."

"But if I turn you, you powers may go. Let's begin with this, can you live forever but without the gifts that power you on to wanting to do this in the first place. I am a scholar of sorts myself and I love feeding up on my own knowledge, but can you do that without having the magic to perform the knowledge." Never trying any magic, I do not know what happens if a magical creature turns, or even if I can do magic myself. Reminding myself there is much I do not know about being a vampire myself, I do not know if keeping your magic so something anyone can do. Being alone and content in the life I lead, discovering more about myself isn't something I have really done, so performing magic is something we might be able to do but is it worth the risk.

"Second, how can you help me if your powers do go? The sphere then will not work for you, and I may get very angry if that happens" Looking at me while I explain my points, I feel in my gut that this speech is more for me than him. He has already made up his mind, it just depends if I am the willing party to do this to him.

"The last and most crucial information I feel I deadly need to give you. Even as a pagan, as a kind ass hunk of a man-"

"Why thank you" He gives me one of his cheeky smiles, brightening his eyes.

"Amara, you are most likely to die. I have only ever truly turned two humans in the past. One an ex-lover who died a painful death brought on by my need for him to join me."

"And the next?" He quizzes his blood doing a leap inside him.

"Eferhild survived. My protégé. She is everything one needs and wants to be as a new vampire but I felt it would work with her, I knew. Changing you now, I feel I am just killing you." Draining my own drink, I honestly do not know how often I can turn people. With no master of my own to teach me, I am self-discovering everything I can about the vampire disease, as the humans call it.

"I am not asking you to turn me tonight. I wish to help you first, gaining the trust and time needed for you to do this to me. My magic is my problem, though this is another reason I wish to do it. I want to research using myself if I do turn and do successfully get to keep my powers and become the most powerful pagan. I feel in my gut that you are meant to be the one to do this to me, making me better, making me powerful. Together we could be unstoppable, and I want the power I feel flowing through you. You have so much to discover, I feel it and I want to be by your side discovering it with you." Holding out his hand onto the table between us, I watch as my hand falls into his without my permission. The draw I feel to him taking over my usually more powerful presences.

"If I help you find and defeat this evil, do you promise to turn me as your pagan night creature?"

"I have on last question for you first." I state, looking deep into his brown eyes with what looks like golden cracks running through them.

"Yes, go ahead"

"Do pagans not believe nature and balance rule the world. Everything has a consequences and a ripple effect on the world around us?"

"No that is Wiccan. They believe all life is sacred and we should cherish it. Witches like pagans follow different views. We believe in a vast array of gods and goddesses and that death and magic are all part of nature. The undead like you, for example the night creatures are a part of nature. So in turn, me becoming one is not a bad thing. It is nature taking me on the next step of my journey. This is why I believe I will keep my gifts and make my gods proud" Moving to his feet, Amara's own brown suit has been perfectly tailored to him, his broad shoulders and chest trying to break out of his shirt and checkered waistcoat.

"Shall we start with the sphere then?" I ask, placing my hand on the cold surface of the fragile object.

"So that is a yes?" He excitingly asks his heart pounding so fast it feels as if my own heart is in my ears.

"I agree yes. I will turn you once I have dealt with this evil, not before. I will not risk your magic leaving you, though in truth I am myself curious to see if you can keep it." I laugh, about to throw the sphere at him. "If you do, could you teach me more? Like the sage as protection?"

"I think we can arrange that. Now put down the sphere carefully, it can break very easily. I do wonder why your Shaman had it in the first place" He ponders as I silently put the sphere back on the table top.

"Why wouldn't he?"

"Spheres are objects of wiccan and pagan magic. More so of mystics or gypsy many call them. Shaman do not often use magically crafted objects. They are more inclined to use handmade items from nature depending on the use." Passing me back the compass, I give him a quizzical look, pondering his choice to give me it. "We will not need this; it is for you alone to have." Raising his hand, he stops my question before I can form it. "I do not know what it is for, all I know is it is for you alone. I cannot open it meaning those carvings on it are of great power, made at a time long ago. Now, let us have the rest of our meal so we can use this sphere." Taking our soup bowls easily, he vanishes back up the stairs before I can call him back.

Back into his office full up on blood, food in his case, the pagan has four books laid out in front of him. The Sphere in the centre of the table, Amara has placed it on a perfect sized silver stand. How he has a stand seeming to have been made alone for this object, I speak no words, only watch as he does his thing.

Every book he has pulled down from his shelves are ones from the last shelf I cannot touch. Trying of course, I stand now leaning against his books on law, their ancient bindings dusting up my new suit.

Asking him why the books are spellbound, Amara informed me he will unbind them from me once I turn him. Not a silly man, he doesn't one hundred percent trust me knowing if I can learn to do this myself, my use for him will vanish very quickly. Unknown to him, his attractiveness and smart attitude are what truly are keeping him alive. Wanting to find out more about him, my intrigue grows the longer I spend in his presence. Finding he is someone I wouldn't mind adding to my already growing protégé list, I know if he can pull this off and find me this evil, I will make his wish come true.

"If you could dim the lights for me?" He asks, his head low over the book closest to him.

"And you guess I can do something like that, because?" I ask back

"Because you have fingers like me, and the dimmer is right next to the candle stick." Stating the obvious, I laugh at myself, assuming that he must know of my powers. Just because you have books written on my kind, doesn't mean they know everything.

"Or you could do, I don't know. Your vampire thing and bring the shadows in around us" Giving me his cheeky smile he's been plastering me with all night, I give him an evil look before doing as he requests.

"Dark enough for you pagan?"

"Just about right. Now, once I begin I cannot stop. And I don't mean do not stop me, I mean I will not be able to stop. Pagan magic can be raw and unpredictable so do not shy when the unexpected happens. Though it may not." Clicking his fingers one by one, I watch as he prepares to ready himself. His lungs expanding as he draws in a long lasting breath, the air in the room grows colder from the stillness washing over him.

"You will not lead the evil to us, this you can promise?" I ask

Shaking his head slowly, his eyes are now closed, while his hands hover over the four books. Clicking his fingers like he did moments ago, I smell burning before I see a thin layer of flames appear over the book pages.

My shadows moving further in to the room as do I, my curiosity sparking at what I am about to witness. The flames on the pages being the only light holding my darkness at bay, the fire looks calm, friendly but dangerous. Power against my own, the flame layers lick at Amara's arms growing as he mumbles words far too quickly for even me to hear.

His left hand moving away from the flames, he picks an item up from out of sight, his hand darting to his other one in one smooth motion. Slashing his forearm through his shirt, he brings his arms over the Sphere, the flames crawling from the books to circle the stand just in front of them. The cream fabric of Amara's shirt dyes marron in a matter of seconds, his right arm releasing scarlet drops down over the fragile object underneath.

My own suit jacket off too, I feel a presence enter the room, brushes past me as it aims for Amara. Flashing in my mind, I see the grey cloud seeping in the street outside, it searching for the prize it has wanted all this time. Reaching its hand up to Amara's home, my vision comes back to the pagan in front of me, a figure now standing behind him. Bones everywhere; the figures face is a deer's skull, its broad antlers coming out of its head scratches at the wood of the shelves on either side of the library.

My body going straight into protective mode, I open my ears up listening for anything from the figure like a heartbeat or a breath. No sound at all, except the mumbling of Amara, I flash around to my new friend's side, pushing all my strength into getting the figure away from my pagan. Vanishing faster than I can even move, the figure appears on the other side of the table The figure blatantly ignoring me in this instance, instead reaches out its human hand to place on Amara's, touching the skin of the man who is my only hope at this time of finding this evil.

Black and brown, the two skins touch lightly, the entities or whatever it is, feeding its power into Amara's spell. Dark skin running up into a long black cloak, I can now feel the god like power pushing in on the room itself. The presence I felt push past me, the power ebbing off this divine power, forces itself onto Amara making him uses the god's power.

Crying out, as his blood turns from a drop to a pour, the blood soaking my sphere begins to turn it red. The flames no longer holding a perfect circle around it, they now lick at the blood covering the sphere, their tongues drinking on the fresh blood given to them. Another flash of grey taking over my mind, I fall back against the bookcase behind me, the force of this vision enveloping my soul. With my suit jacket off and no sage in my waistcoat pocket, I am open to everything this evil wants to throw at me.

Pushing myself off the bookcase, I move myself firm against the back of Amara's chair, refusing to be moved. Like a stake to my heart, my worst nightmare becomes fact as the grey cloud comes into my view.

Crawling along the floor that enters the study like it can go anywhere it wants, I and the god like creature, see the evil coming, his reaction telling me he is afraid of this power too. Within a blink of an eye, his vanishes and reappears next to me, placing one hand on Amara and one hand on me.

Heat far hotter than any fire I have ever remembered feeling in my lifetime, seers down my back, crackling so hard it feels like freezing cold ice taking me over. Every scar covering the whole of my back rips open, my soul showing itself to the God before me. Power in the blood that flows from Amara and me in the room, I see the grey cloud curls its evil fingers up over the tip of the table. The fire from the books attacking the cloud as it shifts and grows forward, I watch as before me the cloud begins to fill up the room before the desk.

The God pushing its power further into me, I feel my mouth begin to mutter, the words I do not understand flowing out of me as they do Amara. Pulling me towards Amara, the God creature's grip digs in deeper, pain seeping out of my body. Pain again, I wonder what this evil could be, the pain I have felt over the last few nights being enough to last me an eternity.

Putting my hand on Amara's other shoulder to the on the entity has it on, I feel the shift of power link between us, the power the three of us have become one as the triangle is made.

Coaxing the grey cloud to seep towards the sphere, the flames attacking the cloud draw it in low, keeping it from trying to touch Amara. As the cloud touches the outer red rim of the sphere, I feel the God's body contract, the power pumping between us three, shifting each time it moves from one body to the next. Sending with it this time, I feel a light grow inside me, the darkness of my own soul merging with the god next to me.

Timing it perfectly and under no control of mine, the power shifts one last time into Amara, giving him just what he needs to complete this spell. One final word leaving his mouth, the pagan smashes his hand down on the sphere, shattering it into a million tiny pieces.

With a gust of wind, the room is swept clean, and everything goes black.

"Cayden?" A deep husky voice calls out to me.

"Amara?" A hand touching the top of mine, I sense the drained body beneath me, Amara's human body going through having a God and night creature's power in him. "I think... I think I saw one of your gods"

"The god LED" Amara tries to say, his voice growing weak from the magic he just performed.

"LED" I nod understanding the name from the tiny part of light I feel dancing around in my body. Power left from the god's visit into my soul. "Did it work?" I ask leaning down so my face is parallel to Amara's. It may be pitch black to him, but to me, I see can clear as day.

"See... for yourself" Breathless words answer me, the smell of his blood sweeping up into my nostrils.

Sat on his soft palm he shows me a tiny ball as big as a marble. Jet black, the marble does nothing as I stare at it, its presence showing me nothing. Seeming to get at what I feel about the ball, Amara moves his hand to the left, then slowly he keeps it moving fully to the right, ending up with his face in mine. Glowing grey, when the ball moves past a point he is turning from, it returns back to its colourless shape, his demonstration making sense to me.

"It will glow grey whenever you are heading in the correct direction. Sort of like the compass in your pocket, yet it will only glow when facing the source of this evil cloud." Giving me another one of his smiles though weaker this time, I cannot help but push him with all my strength, my excitement of it working over powering me.

Falling back out of his chair, I end up above him as he hits the floor hard. "You did it!" I shout down at him, wanting nothing more than to show this man my gratitude for all his. "Thank you pagan"

"You are most welcome." He chuckles, asking if he is allowed to return to his feet.

"Of course, of course. Here" Dragging him up far too quickly, I apologise for my over excitement, the buzz of having all of our powers flowing through us still buzzing through me like a drug.

"I must rest, and you must hunt. You have a promise to keep." Nudging me in the chest, Amara kisses the air at me, my mind doing a flutter at the thought of me joining him back in his bed now he has done this for me.

"I shall keep it indeed. Ball please" I command, holding my hand out.

"Just be careful Cayden, this evil is of nothing I have felt. To have a god intervene and help us in person with this magic, it means this creature you are about to face is not one to be messed with" Warning me, Amara squeezing my hand as we leave his office.

"Till we meet again Amara Aldwin" I nod

"Blessed be Cayden McNigh"

"I never told you my name" I shout back at him as he slowly walks back to his bedroom.

"We are connected now Cayden. If only you would let yourself feel again. Like how you did three hundred years ago. You would feel how deep our connection goes... goodbye sleepless night creature" Feeling the smile I know he has on his face, I watch his bum disappear from view as confusion to what he means swims in the back of my mind.

As a vampire I do not understand what he means by feel it. Vampires feel stronger than any human could possibly try. I feel the light inside me, given by both pagan and his God. But deeper than that. Brushing off his words, I pull out the ball. I have an evil to hunt, and a pagan to keep a promise to but also I have a protégé counting on my getting back to my estate as quickly as I can.

Seven

With the sun long gone, I shift straight into my usual pace of movement. The marble orb in one hand, I follow the route that is easily laid out for me. Who knew finding this evil could be so easy. Luck clearly on my side, I flash to the end of the street, the orb glowing its grey colour to me until I use my speed.

The instant I flash, the grey light also starts flashing, blinking in and out of exist, making me have to turn on the spot, my speed making it give me false directions. Stopping the use of my super speed, I slowly spin on the spot at the end of the street, letting the orb calm down from the fast pace I just took it on. Obvious it doesn't like me using my speed, walking like a human will have to be my only option.

Far from Amara and his illusion of a home, I cannot get him from my mind. Powerful and smart to say the least, how can one human give off such certainty about themselves and their own knowledge. Making me feel like the student, the one who hasn't been around for three hundred years, I feel as if I have been living under a rock. How could I have missed meeting someone like him before, though I get the feeling this meeting of us in some way was always meant to happen.

Yes he can look after himself, but if he had gone to that vampire underground, I have a feeling he would have died. Knowing now after I have successfully turned Eferhild, I know it can be a tricky business and if you do not care much for the person you are changing, the chances of it being successful would be slim.

Someone with his charisma and charm are definitely someone I wouldn't mind being around for the rest of eternity. Meeting a few aged vampires in my time, I have to say I do not get on with most of them. Rare in meeting, I have always kept myself to myself, their rules and life choices irate me on a regular basis.

Luckily for me, most of the ones around now are younger, so in turn are weaker than me. The few that are older, stay locked in their towers of power deep within city limits waiting for their protégé's to bring them food.

Amara, like Eferhild is a being I think I would like to train, to be a part of a family, a colony that is entirely our own. How I have met two figures in the last few days that I want to step into my life forever, I do not know, but as the Shaman might say now I have my old memories of him. Fate is something that seeps into your life in a way that you may not notice, for if you do, luck is on your side to show you the way your life can flow.

Letting fate flow from me now, I squeeze on the orb slightly, readying myself for the fight ahead. What I am about to face I am not sure, but I know I have to win. Not just for me or for the future.

Turning left out of the street, I walk wishing I had a cane to go with my new outfit. Always enjoying the look and the sound a cane makes every time it taps the stone floor, I swing by a young couple of girls, their perfume soaked into their skin to make them more appealing. To be out this late and in this darkness together, they must be working. Feeling sorry for these women at one time, I soon changed that idea when a previous feed of mine told me how many can enjoy this life, the life of a delinquent. Being an elite might not be all it's cracked up to be, after all as a high escort they get to stay in the nicest places alone and with clients.

"Have a good evening ladies" I say as we pass, gaining a few giggles from them.

Moving on, I head forward, following the winding streets, the common fog that seeps into every place on this country now, starts to crawl in around me feet. Quiet, the silence makes me ponder the meaning for the lamplights at this time of night. Most people who want to do harm wait out of sight of the light, meaning if you're heading somewhere alone, these lights won't help you.

A figure for example two feet ahead, stumbles, his breathing heavy and jiggered as he leans on an alleyway entrance. Even a non-supernatural could easily pull him into an alley and rob him blind. The effect alcohol has on the human body is immense. How they haven't worked out that drinking it doesn't help them, but instead hurts them deeply.

Strolling past, I give him a slight push with my finger, helping him fall backwards into the alley. Knocking his head, he passes out instantly, my need to feed calling to me again. Even with Amara's dinner and the last feeds I have had over the past few days, I do not know how much energy I will need for this next fight. This evil with the power to hunt me is not short on power, so doing the only smart thing; I should try and get all I can to fight back.

Sliding into the alley, I grab hold of his jackets collar and pull him deeper into the empty lane. Bricked on all sides with black greasy stones, the alley looks damp just from it being the place where two building wish to be one. Shoulders hefty and broad, this man is pounding with strong blood, the fitness he must do to stay this big and strong taking a lot of training.

Not wanting to get blood on my new outfit, I go for the controlled draining tonight. My anger and fear under control thanks to Amara's sage, I feel a wash of serenity fill me as I hunt like I would on an old normal night.

Ripping the right side of the man's top open, I lean his head to the left, his neck veins rising up to me as the blood calls out. Smooth and ready, his neck looks to rise as I draw near, the vein in his neck wanting me to pierce the skin softly, making as little mess as I can.

Fangs popping out, they ache to bite the skin, drawing the waiting red source to fill my mouth. Like two pins stabbing into soft fabric, my fangs dip deep into the man's layered organ. Waking up as my teeth enter him, he groans a painful sound, his body waking up as I suck on the first few drops of blood.

Crying out, I place my hand that was holding his neck in place over his mouth, leaning my body onto him so he cannot move. Draining slowly, I drink and swallow in mouthfuls of his life, taking the copper substance into my own body.

How it feels to drain another life into yours, feeling every ache they do, shudders into my skin. The pain he feels only fuels me on, draining far slower so I get every shudder I can. Deep and powerful, the demon in me lives off this pain, the power I hold over the victim beneath me.

Choking on the last of his own life, the last minute of energy he has left, the man hits both of his hands out at me, fighting the draw I put into him. My fangs releasing a part of my poison into him, his body soon goes limp halfway through my feed. Not made to be fed so freely from, his body will no longer move, meaning all he can feel is the pain of his soul leaving his body through my hunger and greed.

Sucking deep, I take everything I can get from him, the blood tasting just as sweet as the men who I drained only a few days before. Taking all I can from him, his body is empty by the time I unclasp my fangs.

No drops escaping, or polling around where I bit, I stand wiping my mouth to make certain I have no blood over my face. Clean, I lick my teeth on the inside, my fangs as long and as sharp as they always are. Smiling, I thank the man for his life and own stupidity of strolling the dark streets alone while drunk.

Leaving him where he is, I know this is one hunt I do not have to cover up. If the man is found, no one will suspect a vampire kill, instead they are more than likely to believe he fell down drunk and never got up again. A quiet looking alley like this, means traffic through it is rare, his body will not be discovered for a matter of days.

Exiting the alley, the street has gained some traffic with carts and citizens of the city moving about. Knowing in my gut it is many hours until sunrise, I listen to their breathing seeing why they could be moving about so late.

"Mare will be angry with us for being out so late." A young man sounds off to his companion.

"Your new wife will have to get used to it at some point. We men are like animals, we must feed and drink until our hearts and dicks are content." Grabbing his friends junk, the older man points at a group of woman laughing on an alley corner a few roads away. "The women wait for us, now we must show them a good time."

Punching his mate in the gut, the younger man pulls the cart they are lugging towards the women. His heart pounding at the idea of getting some from anyone but his new bride, how the young are so led by the old. Moving on myself, I slip from this side of the road and dart around an oncoming carriage.

Noises everywhere, I wonder how anyone in any of these buildings could still be sleeping, I mean the sudden rush of people changes this quiet street completely. Considering no one was around only a few moments ago, it shows how city streets grow in crowds within a matter of seconds.

Wrapped up as if she is out for winter, a woman exiting the carriage I just avoided, darting from the safety of her wooden box to the building in-front of her. A butler opening the door, she enters with a dip of her head, meaning this is not her home. How the devils come out at night, especially in a city.

Making me smile, I think about the stories people try to make out about my kind. These humans are the ones who are naughtier than us. As a night creature I hunt to feed. These humans on the other hand break their own rules of society in the dark, all to feel the rush of making a spark in their lives.

Checking my orb, I see the colourless object is giving me nothing. Either way I go down the street the ball will not glow, thought turning to the house the girl just entered, the orb glows its horrid grey colour signalling me to move through a building.

Not in the mood to break in with a busy street around me, I decide to go left down the road. Heading away from the crowd, I circle around to the other side of the building. Moving at a quicker pace, I think I may have found the source; the building she entered could be the one I have been searching for all night.

Mistaken and over enthusiastic, I find my way to the back garden of the hopeful building. Ball glowing again, it wants me to walk down a long dead street with no end in sight, opposite the small garden of the house I thought it could be. Ignoring the building which just happened to be in the way, I push my hopefulness of finding the cloud easily away from my mind.

A funny design for the way these streets have been built, I follow the road, the quietness of this street feeling just like the other one had earlier. Smaller buildings here this is more of a residential street, giving me the feeling the orb is taking me on a wild walk about. How do I know that the pagan hasn't performed a spell that has me wander the city while the grey cloud can come find me. Trusting in someone so easily, either though I was part of the spell, felt the spell, felt the god. Everything in my mind warns me to be careful of this pagan, but my heart and body want to fully let him take control.

Sounding off to the left, I hear a break shatter across the floor. Confused by the sound making so much noise without a human sounding panicked alongside it, I put the orb away. If a human had done something to make a loud enough noise like that, a panic breath or muttering would follow straight after.

Flashing towards where the sound has come from, I stand at the end of a small front garden, the tiny gate to enter it pushed off his hinges lying on the floor in a heap. Broken wood hanging on the brick wall, I hunch down to look at where the gate came off.

From the break in the wood, something very strong and very fast flew through the gate, the object or being not stopping even when they came into contact with the small wooden protector. Reaching my finger out to the gate, my mind gains a massive flash of grey, the power of the cloud rushing back into my head. Falling back onto my bum, my head seers in pain, the power banging against my skull as it tries to take over my mind. Ramming my hand down onto the sage in my pocket, I pull it up to my nose taking in a huge human breath to protect myself.

Breathing in and out, just like when I was in the bed, my head pounds as the protection fights against the evil coming for me. Knowing for sure where I now am, I open my eyes, the darkness around me hurting as my head steadies itself. Needing the sage to burn to gain more protection, I take one last draw from its smell before putting it away. Needing it for long term use, I know I cannot burn it away or risk losing my protection altogether.

The ground damp from the cold night air, I take a real look at the garden. Ripped and attacked, the garden beds have been torn away as the main tree in the centre of the tiny front now leans into the where the front window of the house should be. Noticing the broken glass from the window and front door, I see where the loud shattering noise came from.

What creature would freak out this much at a garden, even with the grey cloud covering this whole area. Pulling the orb back out, I aim it at the home hoping it will glow to tell me whatever evil I need to face, it's going to be in here.

Colourless, just like it would be, my ears pick up a panicked breath coming from inside the house. Human in origin, its lungs fill and un-fill at an alarming rate, meaning the thing that has destroyed this garden is deep inside this home.

Entering the house silently, I step over the broken door, watching my feet as I step carefully over any broken glass. Not wanting to sound off who I am to the intruder inside, I listen out for movement seeing if there is anything I need to notice.

The living room is wrecked, every piece of furniture looks as if it has been thrown against the wall, the creature who has done this has wanted to make as much mess as it can. Pure anger, the walls have scratches running down the length of them. The mirror from over the fireplace having been punched so many times a huge hole in the wall behind the frame is also destroyed, the strength it would take to do that for a human would leave blood everywhere but here, there is no sign or smell of blood. Following my nose, I sniff the scent of blood further in the home.

Moving through to the kitchen, I see that the creature has moved upstairs. Blood soaking every broken space in this room, pieces of a body have been ripped apart, the actually flesh having been bitten on as a quarter piece of the upper body lays squished next to the oven. Hand and foot prints covering the blood soaked floor, the scene before me tells me whoever did this is of human form. Looking at the body pieces, they are so ripped apart I cannot even tell what they were originally, the single brown slipper being the only clue that this human was a male.

Flashing to the stairway, I stand at the bottom, listening to the pounding of the human still managing to be alive. Rising up, I move up the tattered steps that have not been looked after well. This family living here obviously are not rich, their money going solely on food supplies to survive, than doing up their home.

A scream splintering in through the air, I feel in my heart that the creature has found its prey. Flashing up the rest of the stairs I dart to the screams, the pain coming from the woman being my only way to know where I need to go.

Bursting in through a side door, the killer hasn't used; I enter a broken room full of dust. Tattered fabrics hang everywhere while, a single mattress lays on the floor. A woman lying on the mattress in pure destress, the creature I am looking for sits on top of her, its own clothes in rich tatters.

Too late to save her, even though that is not my reason for being here, her last scream rips through the sound barrier of the universe as the monster on her rips her guts out. Drinking on the blood that spurts out into the world, the woman's body convulses under the mindless creature driven solely on devouring the human beneath it. Its nails long and sharp cut in the human, ripping her apart as it feeds on any part of blood it can find. Hungry for as much as it can get, the monster dives its head into human, a feral creature driven completely on blood and destruction.

Letting it do what it needs to, I watch analysing this night creature and the animal is has become. Far worse than an animal really, this creature is doing something even a lion wouldn't do. Wasting a lot of blood and eating parts it doesn't need, this creature has no plan in what it is doing. Not even driven by bloodlust, the creature is driven mad with fire. Wanting to destroy and destroy alone. Forgetting the body it was attacking it goes for the mattress underneath her digging through her body to just destroy its next find.

Ripping at the red died fabrics, it even uses its teeth to attack the bed, its back to me, I feel as if I am watching a puppy play with a toy for the first time. Growling and snuffling, I would say this creature is more wolf than one of my kind. What has become of him I am not sure, though all I do know is the grey cloud is written all over this.

Coughing loudly enough to make it over his animal craze, I lean on the door frame, wondering how he is going to react to me.

Head snapping round, I step back shocked at who I see. Far older than I can even imagine being, the creature before me is not just anyone. A night creature of legend the animal before me stares into my eyes, the memory of him commanding his protégés to rip at my back clouding my mind.

Standing in a court of vampires, the beings around me are regal and hard. Sent here as punishment for resenting the way I was turned, for the way my master wanted to teach me about our kind I see every pair of eyes staring down at me from the high seating on both sides of me.

Killing my master out of spite, the oldest night creature made from what seems like crystal with how hard he holds himself, the vampire before me holds his court strong. Free and happy, this master hated mine for wanting to live apart from them. Choosing his own path once they were turned together, the rule the one before me has created is fed off of blood and hierarchy. The highest anyone can be, he is the strongest in this court, the most feared and respected. Anything he asks of his protégés will be passed out no matter the quest and harshly.

"Young one, you have been charged with being turned outside of the confines of our way. Your undead life was not of your master's choice to perform, and as such you should not exist this way. Enternal death has been judge and tried to your master life... for you a punishment for allowing his dark lure to change you shall be slashing for the next five years. One year for every thousand years your master lived on this planet." His cold colourless eyes shining down on me from his high seated chamber, my punishment started, two days after I was turned into a night creature.

"I have not been clouded, you are the clouded ones. For turning me, for making me one of you, you have murdered your own, killed another master of your kind for wanting to have a family of his own." I speak out, as two protégés take my arms pushing me down to my knees. "He was your brother, born of the same human woman, born from the first ever night creature to ever exist in this world. You punish him for not wanting to live under his older brother's rule forever, for wanting one person to spend his time with. One child for him to have as his own?" I beg, asking the question I know I will not understand the answer to.

"You are of no consequence in the past I had with my youngling of a brother. I am the head of the vampires and you will learn to respect my authority. He died disobeying his leader and for you this is your one chance of joining us, the one single mercy I will give a new night creature brought into this would wrongly. The first and only true vampire set these rules that no vampire may die at the hands of another, for the sins of another. My brother has died for his sins; do not create your own before your undead life has begun." Clapping his hands loudly, he stops any comeback from me by stinging my new heightened hearing.

"Valdin and Velen, my newest night creatures. Begin the punishment" Waving his hand to start the entertainment, the pain of the first nails entering my skin, burned like lava being poured onto my bare back.

His white eyes gleaming at me, I watch the oldest vampire stare at me in joy, as every piece of pain was placed upon me for five straight years.

My memory and mind clearing, the oldest vampire still stares at me, his eyes piecing every part of my soul.

"Volmir" I stutter, the pain of my scars ripping up my back as I say his name.

"Ahhhh" He screams, his body flying at me through the air so quickly I have not time to flash out of the way.

Pushing me out into the hall, we fall down the stairs, our bodies rolling over one another. The smell steaming off him is of death and piss, the feralness crying out of him in everything he does. His head flashes back and forth as we fall, I feel the grey cloud seeping back into my mind, this crazed creature ready to rip me apart. His clothes torn apart from his own rage, I kick him off me as we land at the bottom of the stairs, his mad mind sending him running off into the street, not truly caring for a fight.

Eight

Volmir the oldest of us mad, how can this be. Cold, hard and with the need to always be right, I would never put the creature running out of my sight, next to the one who sits in his courtroom so proudly. A few days is all I knew of my master but it was all I needed to know how caring he was. How two brothers came be so far from each other, it astonishes me.

Finding no fixed memories in my mind of my human life, all I can feel are pieces, things I know because I was human, feelings I had. Now, well I feel curious, intrigued to find out where my old punisher will go to.

Pushing myself up to my feet, I flash out of the house, catching the last glimpse of Volmir turning away from the direction I came in with my orb. Passing all the houses left, I wonder what he's hunting, what is driving him to kill. Is the grey cloud doing all of this, making him pass these houses or is he just burning off energy flushing through himself.

Running at a jog, I manage to keep a good pace and distance between us. Looking as if he is sniffing out a secret I can't see myself, he darts from one side of the road to the other, his mind making him smash anything in his way. Whether it be a lamppost or a wall, Volmir's hardened skin lets him blast through anything he wants.

Seeming to kind of enjoy the destruction, I wonder if it's relieving him of the anger clouding his mind. Feeling the crushing sensation pounding into my own head only a few minutes ago, I can't help but feel pity for the cold creature that gave no mercy to me in the past.

Stopping dead, I sidestep against a wall pulling even more shadows down around me so I am completely hidden. Doing so just in time, Volmir spins on the spot looking hard at the spot I was in a second before. Moving his head, his body seems to be stuck shaking constantly, it wanting anything to hurt at all times.

Flashing up next to me on the street, he ignores the wall I am hidden upon on, but instead walks back the way we just came. Flashing across the road, he begins smashing up another garden, ripping up any plant life he can find. Picking up a bird bath, he raises it over his head to then throw it, the concrete object crashing into the wall above my head.

Flashing to the right, before the dust coming of the destroyed bowl can make me dirtier; I now hide myself behind a front garden fence. Crazed and wild, he smacks his head against the new front door he is at, opening it instantly. Confusing me further, Volmir starts gagging, dropping to his knees as his body starts convulsing like the dead woman that was beneath him. Coughing and gagging harder, he spews up the human remains he just devoured, his body rejecting the items it does not need.

Vampires as a species do not need to eat raw food or at least our bodies do not like it. Rejecting it as would a human body would, this is the repercussions of whatever the grey cloud is doing to this night creature, killing him slowly.

Empty and much rawer than he was before; Volmir moves his head again listening out for something. Forgetting the house he is standing at, his flashes off, heading down the road I entered here on. The human of the garden Volmir was just destroying exits his house in a daze, his face a horror at the new sight before him.

Following Volmir once again without the human noticing my presence, I leave the human to wonder what could have happened to his home, his lucky escape from being massacred only just coming. Volmir flashing away, I flash too aiming for where I think he is going, where I hear the sound signalling to.

Standing at the end of the street I was on only some time ago, people seem to have flocked here, the reasoning becoming apparent with something I missed earlier. A local pub avoiding my view when I was distracted by the food I had, the cream coloured building explains the drunken man I fed off, and how he was so drunk on a quiet street alone. So men finishing work earlier than others mean they get drunk far quicker than others having the bar to themselves, now with all the people in the street, I see the prime time for the pub is in full swing.

The local whores all dressed and ready for business stand on the corner of the street where the road splits of into two directions, the pub called the old flame in the centre of where the road divides. Its light the main attraction of the street, I see the two men I listened to earlier are still chatting up some of the whores, like they might get a free ride. How the human mind believes it's going to get what it wants with just an utter of a few nice words, has always made me chuckle. The scene now unfolding in front of me worries me for my own kind, for the kind I have just turned Eferhild into.

Starting close to me, Volmir, darts up to the first person he finds on the street. A young woman dressed well for the type of area she is in, she looks younger than anyone else in the street, her first time out whoring perhaps. Petit and with a jump in her step, I feel bad she is the first person Volmir starts upon.

Calling the shadows to me, I move against the tallest building in the street, a perfect place to watch the terror unfold. It may be cruel and mean, but if I am honest, the death of these humans standing around will not pull on my heart strings. I only worry that a single survivor may get away and tell the world of what they witness, not that anyone will believe them, this could be the moment my kind is truly discovered in this world.

Attacking her openly, he stabs into her chest and pulls out not her heart but her ribs. Looking like he has just taken a pair of wings from her, they shine whiter than an angel before blood begins to pour from her back. Holding her body up, Volmir yanks her head to the side and moves in for his first bite. Gorging deep, he bites again and again, making the girl's blood spurt up over his already blood covered body.

Moving so quickly that the girl didn't have time to scream, only one person has begun to notice, his face moulding, creasing in confusing. The young man does not make a sound, not understanding what is happening before him or if this is a street art show of some kind.

Laughter barking off a group of men leaving the local pub, the one man who has noticed the vampire turns to the street before him, signalling so his attention is taken by the group. Foolish, as in the moment he notices what is happening he could have run, it is certain now he will certainly be Volmir's next victim.

Dropping the girl's body, Volmir flashes to the man who was watching yanking his left arm off. Putting his face where in place of the arm, he drinks the oozing blood as the man screams out, the world around Volmir becoming aware of his presence.

Screams echoing down the street, the group of whores seeing what is going on cannot contain their horror. All the men in the street do exactly what the dying man just did. All so brave and foolish, they think the women are being hysterical and silly, shushing them. The two men I saw earlier move over to their cart to get a better look at what is happening.

Draining as much blood as he wants from this victim, Volmir than shoves his face into the open wound, eating much of it as the man losses consciousness. His body dropping in a lump, Volmir first starts to go with it, before his attention is drawn away by a man scurrying up onto a carriage a foot down the road. The panic coming off of him, he takes Volmir's full draw, making the night creature act like a lion in the midst of a full hunt.

Flashing to the man's carriage, he rips the door and first wheel off easily, his pure strength bursting free at the object in front of him. Screaming out, a couple inside the carriage stare out at the face of death, both the men inside have their trousers down around their ankles. Death coming to greet them while they were in the act of lust, one man falls out of the carriage through the other door. Climbing slowly up into the carriage, Volmir greets the whole street with the shouts of pain his show being the only thing anyone on the street is now watching. The man on top, who brought Volmir's attention to the carriage, jumps back off the carriage and running like a hellhound towards the pub, leaving his employers far behind.

Trousers still around his ankles, the man who fell from the carriage is young, wearing not so very nice clothing. Telling me that he is not the owner of the carriage, this boy does the smartest thing any human has done tonight. Running past me, he flees into the streets of the city finding an escape while the crowd stands still waiting to see what Volmir does next.

Done with the person inside, Volmir flashes out of the carriage, chasing a hobbling man who has decided to try darting past where I am hidden. Pushing himself up into the air in a high jump, Volmir comes down hard on the man, squishing his body into the cobbles below. Breaking his arms as he tries to stop the fall, the strength behind Volmir's jump is too much for the human man.

Turning to see the rest of the street again, more people seem to have appeared, coming out of the local buildings and of course the pub. The whores no longer in sight, I see that every person in the crowded street is male, them all taking a united front.

Still only watching for now, they all seem to think if they hold strong, Volmir may flee from his desire to eat, to kill. Fools that they are, I know that the lust flowing in his mind means this party stood before him is just what he wants, needs even. For what I can see from this grey clouds power it is making the oldest of my kind turn into what animal humans think we are, mindless killers.

A smacking sound coming from my other side, Volmir has thrown the body of the now dead man against the wall next to me. The body hitting so hard it has imbedded itself against the bricks; making me check my suit that he hasn't covered me in muck.

His head moving again, just like when he heard the street from where we were, the growing crowd has taken his attention again. Flashing up to the first person in the group, Volmir pulls him away making all the other strong men jump back together in fear. Not so strong when he actually comes near them, I can see the collective fear growing within the humans, all too proud to actually turn and flee.

"He is a vampire!" One exclaims, his face flushed with alcohol reddened cheeks.

"Vampires don't exist!" A man shouts from the back of the group, clearly hiding himself in case the night creature comes back at them.

"How do you explain this then Geffrey" A group of the men ask, shoving the man who shouted forward to view the horror of one of the men begging for help as Volmir rips into his sternum.

"What is he doing? Hey leave him alone" Two of the guys spit at Volmir. Stepping up, they hold nothing in their hands; clearly thinking they are strong enough to go up against a vampire so engrossed in his food that he doesn't care they are all watching.

One going in for a punch, his fist hits the vampire's face hard, breaking on impact. Shattering like a sheet of glass, I hear every bone break into tiny pieces, the second man dragging his friend back as Volmir turns his attention to them. Red seeping from his mouth and nails, the monster in front of them answers all their fears of what he truly is. Vampires are real and he is here for all of them.

"We need fire!" One of the men, who have broken off from the crowd, shouts into the pub.

Hearing a bang followed by other noises in the building, the street has grown so quiet, the only nose coming from Volmir as he growls at the men. Stepping forward by one step, Volmir tests their reflexes seeing what they may have up their sleeves.

Moving my vision back on the pub, I hear more banging as the man who shouted in the pub has vanished inside. The door reaching open, the whores from the street spill back out all carrying what look like big pieces of wood. Either from tables or chairs, the wood is passed to the men, making sure everyone has one.

Coming out of the pub after the women, the man who shouted inside for fire, calls to his young friend, demanding he bring their cart to him. Seeing it's the two men who walked past me earlier, I wonder if the older one has heard tales of my kind, knowing fire is their only chance at stopping this powerful angry vampire.

The whore, standing furthest from the night creature, passes the wood to the men, making sure very man who is able, has two pieces. Volmir, mad as he is, darts at the closest men, them all jumping back, away from the vampire except the one. The one with the broken hand isn't very lucky; his body only feeling the pain from his hand. Grabbing him with his super speed, Volmir pulls the unfortunate man off down the street so he can do what he wants with him.

The men with the cart, by the help of the landlord, light the cart on fire, the fabric in it setting instantly. Putting the heads of the wood they themselves hold in, the tables legs light ablaze, sending new light up on the walls around the street. The whores joining them, also light their chair legs, fire coming into this world in an army of citizens not allowing a demon from stories to take all their lives.

Distracted by the humans he has in his grasp, Volmir has managed to get hold of another two men, ripping their arms off in a rage. Flashing back to the man with the broken hand, Volmir has nearly drunk him dry, leaving only a part of the man's life left. His nails long and sharp, Volmir stabs his hands into man's stomach pulling on the intestines waiting inside. Coming out like a snake being yank from a tree, the man's guts wobble in the vampire's hand as the creature bites down on them.

Gasping in horror at the show in front of them, the humans gather in waves as more people empty onto the street. The buildings all around are woken up further as some of the whores run inside them demanding help from the people watching inside. Pulling shadows further down around me, I do not want to exist, or even allow people to believe I exist right now. Not wanting them to spot me or my eyes up close, I make it as if my part of the world has never truly been here in the first place. Shrouded in such blackness, I have become a black hole, ready to destroy anything that comes at me, but not harming anyone out of my range.

What this grey cloud is doing to Volmir, what it will do to me if it gets me. With so many witnesses, the world will hear of this attack. This sighting and continued murders will not go unnoticed. The death and mystery shielding my kind from knowledge is no more, from this night, the myth of my kind will become fact.

Unless of course someone is able to convince each individual person now here, that there is an obvious explanation that isn't supernatural related. With no choice but to stay where I am for now, I know I will not be the person to right this reveal, this horror show can and will be covered up by Volmir's children, his army. But what will become of my kind and their society I am not sure, all I know is the grey cloud will not get me. I will not end up like this old vampire.

Eyes darting left and right as Volmir flashes between the bodies of the men he has ripped the arms off of, I feel like I am watching a group of dancers in action. While others step forward, flames in hand, others move back to the flaming cart, a synchronised movement of fire starting as Volmir pays no attention.

With no worry for his own safety and care of the world, Volmir carries on ripping and biting people apart. Still flashing towards the crowd, Volmir grabs a man by the leg dragging him along the floor to where his other bodies lay. His newest victim even had a flame ready to be used, yet taken by surprise his flame fell behind him. Dragging his latest victims while flashing away has left a deep red line all along the cobbles.

Blood seeping from the back of the new victim, he doesn't scream out for long before Volmir bites his throat out, spraying more blood in the world.

Being a vampire myself, many would assume I would enjoy this show, which in part I do. However the playing with people and mainly drinking of their blood is much more satisfying than the eating of body parts our bodies cannot digest. If the humans wait long enough, his over indulging will end up with him wrenching and falling over, his sick giving them the perfect chance to hurt him.

Strength in numbers, they do not listen to my telepathic power that doesn't exist and the step into their own plan. All with fire ready to protect themselves, they hold them out in front making their fires flame higher. Keeping even Volmir and his feral range in check, he hovers over the bodies he's done with, waiting for his next snack to make a wrong move.

Moving in a formation I have never seen humans naturally do unless they are in a real war, the people spread out in one flow. The closest men to Volmir circle around behind him as the men behind them step forward filling the now empty spaces up quickly.

Side by side, body next to body, the humans circle Volmir easily their fire sticks ready to do their evil bidding of killing a monster. So many of them, they stand in four lines of warriors, each person behind the last holding a flame.

Still not waiting for Volmir's body to wrench, they all hold out their fire stick at arm's length, stretching out towards the vampire. His ancient body going rigid as he looks to give up, the craze in his eyes dwelling slightly as the pain of heat starts to touch his body.

Not being able to fly as an escape away from the attacking humans, I know that the only night creature that could was the true night creature. Long gone, I see the terror coming into Volmir's eyes as death creeps up to him. All the blood he has soaked himself in begins to cook, the blood being a sort of cooking oil while the human oven closes in on all sides.

Pushing off of the ground hard and clumsy, Volmir does the thing I have been waiting for him to do this whole time. Trying to flee now they are all around him, the insane creature falls down on top of the first row back of his oven making a tiny split in the crowd only a fully aware vampire would notice.

Stabbing out hard and fast, all the humans join in, manoeuvring around so each person can get a stab at the cold creature murdering in their street. Keeping the killings quiet and cleaned up so only a few know the truth of the vampires, I feel the hate every person standing in this circle has for my kind now. The monsters from their dreams, I watch as Volmir's body surprisingly takes longer than I thought it would to take light.

Blazing its brilliant and terrifying orange glow on the darkness around it, the flames finally take hold of Volmir; his weakened body from the pure flames around him finally giving up. Starting out as the orange colour of a normal flame, the fire takes hold of Volmir's soul, shifting its colour to a shade of blue. Volmir's poison exiting his body as the fire eats him alive, I watch as the colour of my race calls out to the night world everywhere.

Screaming bloody murder all on his own, Volmir's crazed mind and terror of his own death sounds off into the sky. Fire being one of the only true ways a human can defeat a vampire one to one; the huge crowd of humans wanting to burn a vampire was never going to end with him escaping.

Fire covering every inch of his night creature body, the flames looks to swish into swirls as the fire sparks off, the eyes of Volmir staring at my location. His pure white eyes somehow finding me, they send a shiver of agony down my back as the feeling I knew him before I was a vampire comes into my head.

The flames meeting his eyes, he gives of one massive animalistic roar before the flames licking him to death turn a brilliant black, a crystalized effect coming off of them. I feel the night mourning a death of one of its creatures, its own anguish at the death of one of my kind screaming out at me.

Smoke floating up into the cloudless sky, it look like any normal smoke does. Only this time, the smoke brightens up as Volmir's body drops to the ground, his death claiming him in victory. Raw and cold, Volmir's body continues to feed the fire, the smoke coming off the body beginning to shift into my nemeses of the grey cloud.

The brightening up smoke joins with the wisp of grey cloud that has started to come out of the Volmir's dead mouth. Job done, yet angry because it knows there are more of us night creatures, my body freezing even harder at the sight as the real hunting cloud shows itself to me once again.

Digging my nails deep into the bricks behind me, I stab in hard, my body working quickly to get me away from the thing that has been hunting me this whole time. Knowing in my gut that this isn't the evil that is after me, yet the power that it possesses, I know I still have hunting to do.

Sage still in my pocket, I hope it will protect me fully as I hold the shadows hard against my being, my body rising up away from the watching crowd looking for more of my kind to hunt. Still circling Volmir's body, I move with my eyes still on the scene below, one man steps out of the group to kick Volmir's body turning it into ash on impact.

With no sign the oldest vampire was even here, the grey cloud wisps away in the opposite direction to me, hunting for its next victim. Making it to the top of a tall flat topped building I have managed to climb up backwards onto, a blacker than death raven kraa's at me. Its odd bright Viking blue eyes look me up and down, before it jumps off the building, circling down to look at the commotion below. Falling further back onto the roof, the edgy feeling of fear and anger at the grey cloud are coming back, my neck crinkling as if something is behind me.

"Well what a surprise..." A raspy male voice sounds in my ears.

"Cayden McNigh... what are the chance you have appeared" A squeaky woman adds, my hate for these two creatures making my night even better.

Nine

Flashing to my feet as I spin on the spot, Volmir's favourite pets stand like statues before me. Kraaing as it returns, the raven with the Viking Blue eyes, lands on the opposite building watching us as I greet these night creatures in return.

"Valdin and Velen. Just the vampires I wanted to bump into" I comment sarcastically.

 "Being rude is not a good idea right now McNigh… I am very upset" Velen hisses, her high voice stabbing into my eardrum.

"Why would that be?" I joke, having had enough of playing nice whenever I bump into these two.

Always together and tied at the hip, these creatures that don't really have a mind of their own appear to me whenever I do not need them around. Always out to do Volmir's bidding, they follow him around or go where they are told without question. In three hundred years neither of them has ever thought of going off alone and seeing what life they could make for themselves.

Twins, they are identical in every way except gender. Impossible I know, but the shape of their faces and the angle of their eyes match so perfectly that they look like neither gender. Apart from the sound of their voices being different, the way in which they pronounce their speech is the same.

Black hair that runs down to their, waists neither has it up, going for the dead straight look. Black eyes apart from the vampire glow of their iris, these two creatures couldn't look any more like a pair of typical vampires if they tried. Long black coats, made of leather so tight if they were human they wouldn't be able to breath. Wrapped around the middle with a tight metal clip, their clothing shows both of them have no body muscle to speak of.

Bringing me out of my analysis of them, Valdin speaks in a voice of hurt, surprising me slightly.

"You… y-you were down t-there. You saw what those filthy humans did to him."

"Oh you mean your lord and master" I laugh out loud, making sure every sound coming out of my mouth echoes in the open air.

"Your master too Cayden" Velen tries to correct me.

"My master?" I quiz, creasing my perfectly smooth forehead at her. "My master was murdered two days after I was changed. I may not remember much about my creation, though I know he did it."

Laughing themselves, they both cut off their sound in the same cold moment, sending a kind of chill down my spine.

"That is what Volmir wanted you to believe. He needed a reason to kill your master and in using you he had one."

"Volmir was your true master" Valdin states, clearly believing himself what he says.

"Then why would my master tell me different? I was there; I remember the conversation on how I became me when I woke. What would Mikal get out of lying to me?" Saying my master's name for the first time in a few hundred years makes my heart ache. The lies they are trying to fool me into believing make me die. I know I do not have memories of being human or changing, but I remember the conversations with Mikal, I know the real truth of my rebirth.

"Do you not remember the first rule about a master being a master? They can tell their protégés to do anything they want; they can change memories in their mind if they want. They have full and sole control over the creatures they have created. You, my naïve vampire, are the grand example of how strong a master's power is" Now being a master myself, I know the power I could have over Eferhild if I want to, I feel the gift that I could control her, manipulate her into whatever I want but I know the connection I had with my master was real, just as I know the connection with Eferhild is real.

I know the Shaman was able to hide our past together from me, but I feel in my gut that I would know if Volmir was my master. Take tonight, when I found him when I saw him, the memory that came back to me was of our first true meeting, the meeting in which these two creatures before me started ripping my back apart. If Volmir was my true master I would have felt the pull I get for Eferhild when I'm near her, I would feel the creature he is truly to me.

"Did Volmir tell you this truth?" I ask putting a pretend weakness into my voice for them.

"He did. After your five years of torment, he confided in us the truth of who you were. The person you where before you were turned and who you were to us. Wiping you from our mind too, I was as shocked as you are now about who you are Cayden" Velen's irritable voice tells me, her acting is incredible.

"And who am I to you both?" I ask my belief in their words being as low as a fly on the food chain.

"You're our cousin Cayden. Your true name is Vilanom and we all grew up together" Valdin words wash right by my ears, the lies they seem to believe if they do, are quite hilarious.

"I'm sorry but you are both of Japanese descent... I am clearly not." I say motioning down at my own body.

"Cousin you fool... not brother. It is entirely possible for you to be a cousin with our family moving over to this country." Velen hisses again, seeing I am not as fooled as I was pretending.

"Your master has just died so I grant you the pain you feel. I myself have felt it too, only my master was only around for two days. How it must feel to be with him, following every command and not questioning anything because he wouldn't allow it. It must be truly hard, for what do you do now? Now he has burned, crisped up so much he is now ash and you are both alone, stuck in a place in our world where your lives have no meaning. Your position in the court is not of high standing without Volmir, the oldest of our race. You are now like me, one of the younglings expected to never speak and exist if they others of the court allow it." Hitting them where I know every word will hurt them; the knife I dig in cannot go in far enough for my liking.

Seething, both of them hold their statue status even though I see the anger burning inside their eyes, blazing towards me.

"Do not fear, for I believe your master died not truly feeling what was happening to him. The pain flowing through him was coming from anger and wildness, things he was never in his life. With the longevity of his life maybe this is what becomes of us. Maybe we shift back into a wild animal like form and kill until we are killed ourselves?" I question them, knowing that is not the case.

Wondering if either of them knows about the grey cloud and the power it is having over our kind, I wait moving my head to see what their respond to my mild kindness of an explanation will be. With the way I have bashed their master and his lies, I think the kindness I have just shown will not go far in helping me get away from these creatures easily.

"You do not understand the world we live in at all do you."

"I understand that you did not try to save your lord and master, yet instead let him die. He was in a quiet street not far from here, the perfect opportunity for you to save him, yet you did not. He is now dead because of you both" I give one of the pagan's cheeky smiles getting myself ready to leave this conversation.

"You are the one who did not save him you coward. We saw how you crawled up onto this roof, covered in shadows, hidden from the humans and their diseases on life."

"You mean the lives that if they didn't have you wouldn't be alive" I counter Velen, growing tired of her voice. "Yes I did crawl up this wall away from the humans who were brave enough to go after one of us... though it isn't the only thing I was getting away from."

"And what else was that cousin?" Valdin asks, looking like he is actually curious to see what I say.

"For the last time Valdin I am not your cousin. If we were cousin do you not think they're would be some parts of us that are recognisable? Even tiny things like the same nose or shape of the mouth."

"Your mother was Scottish Cayden, you are from the highlands. Their blood has overtaken your Japanese blood that is why."

"So my father was Japanese according to you?"

"No your great grandfather was Japanese, which is why you do not look similar to us." Velen tells me, clearly fully believing the lie Volmir has placed in their heads. Why he would want them to not feel the need to hurt me, make me a part of their family. I am not sure, but I do know that I am at the end of this conversation. My time on this roof is coming to an end and the grey cloud of evil is waiting for me to find it. These two will not be any help and telling them of this evil will not help either.

"Your explanation of how a master can rule over his protégés even after his life is gone shows how much power a master truly has. I will never rule my protégés like this but I wish you both to move past his power. I do not wish to fight you but if I have to, I will."

"Fight us! Ha ha ha! You think you could take both of us on? You wouldn't survive if only one of us was here" Valdin states, his laughter continuing even after he stops speaking.

"You are not my issue on this night, so do not make yourselves one. Mourn your master, but find someone, a Shaman maybe that can clear the fog Volmir has placed on your minds. I shall be leaving now, so do not try and stop me" I warn them, my body shaking with the need to flash onto the next roof. The only one in this area that is flat, the others around us are designed like any Victorian building with a slanted roof, meaning if I am to fight, I would wish to do it here.

"Cayden do not be foolish, we are stronger than you" Velen's voice flies to my ears.

"We wish for you to join us… together we shall avenge Volmir and begin our own rule" Closing my eyes to Valdin's words, I ready myself to fight. This night will not be my last but stepping into this could go so very wrong.

Three hundred years in age also, I know these two were changed around the same time as me. Being Volmir's newest protégés when I was chained in his court room, they were given the job of punishing me for five years, making it a sort of punishment for them too. Yes they could hurt me like any vampire can do to another but I am at a similar strength to them now, if not stronger.

Living my own life away from the rule of the master means I have trained myself in how I want to fight, meaning I am a rare difference to them. They do not know my fighting style or power like they do the others of the court. Training with younglings of our age when they grew in power, I trained alone, feeding off of whatever I have wanted over the years.

Moving forward with my eyes closed, I use my senses around me to help in their presence. Sliding down onto the floor, I flash toward Velen first, making my move on the one whose voice drives me insane. From the start she would talk and talk and talk while punishing me, I have only ever wanted to punch her teeth out.

Taking her by surprise because I had my eyes closed, I swipe her feet from under her, my slide stopping so I am at her face when she hits the floor. Hitting out fast and hard, I land my fist into her front teeth, breaking off her fangs in one move.

Crying out in pain and blood she flashes in a spin herself, turning so she can kick me away from her. Her feet digging into my side, I am pushed towards her brother, his anger at my attack them coming off in an aura of darkness.

How dare I attack them and break his sisters teeth, he must be thinking as he reaches down quickly to lift me in the air. Planning on throwing me over the building, I feel his nails dig into my chest and stomach as he grips me ready.

Throwing out my own arms as a reflex, I stab his arms with my own sharp nails using the momentum of him lifting me up towards him to bring my legs up to his face. Ruining my new favourite suit, I kick out at his face, the pain he isn't used to feeling making him release me from his stabbing grip.

Dropped to the floor, I roll away, flashing to my feet, while Velen flies at me, blue blood pouring from her mouth.

"You're bleeding a little Velen" I say as she grabs the front of my waistcoat.

"You'll die for that Cayden" Using all the strength she can find, she yanks me off the ground aiming to do what her brother was also going to do.

Letting my clothes go as I fly through the air, I see the raven again, flapping its wings as it flies away, no longer concerned with what us three vampires are doing. Feeling as if I have flown before in a past life, I reach out my hands out to the floor, the height Velen was hoping to throw me up into the air with doesn't lift me high at all.

Grinding to a stop, my hands have made scratch marks in the roof stonework, the cement now has my mark in it forever. Looking up, I give them both a smile, laughing at how they think throwing me off a building will even kill me. I'm a vampire after all, not one of the humans they get sent out to kill for making a fuss about our race.

"Throwing me from a building will not kill me. Or do you not fight other vampires often enough to know what can hurt our own kind?" I ask mocking them.

"Oh we know. But the fall will hurt you enough that we can take you to where we need to go" Valdin says.

"But Velen says I'm going to die for what I did to her"

"Oh you'll wish you had died... but we need you on our side, so you will join us one way or another" Darting at me, Velen throws everything into coming for me, her quickness, surprising me because even though she is moving faster than sight, I feel the world slowing down so I can move nicely into the right position to grab what I need too.

A gift revealing itself to me, I see everything perfectly in slow motion, my flashing power extending to the world around me slowing down. Any vampire using their flashing speed doesn't slow down time, instead they can move to where they want to, doing what they need to but our minds are on high alert moving at the quick pace our bodies are. This, what is happening right now is different, I feel so aware of the time passing by me, I feel on instinct that I am controlling the speed of life around me, of time itself.

Knowing I do not understand everything that a vampire is capable of, I also know no vampire alive today understands all of what we as a species can do. Wrapping my hand slowly into Velen's hair as she moves, continuing the attack she thinks she is about to hit, I see neither of these two night creatures have tapped into the power I am now using. Coming to me in the need of it, my instincts let me use a power that I did not know I have. Learning as time goes on, I know this is one power I will not be afraid of using again.

Time speeding back up, I yank on Velen's hair pulling her so she stands in front of me as Valdin thrust forward landing his punch of an attack into Velen's already broken face. As she cries out I pull on her hair again, bringing her down to the ground where I stab at her throat with my nails, digging in four quick times, to make her choke like a human would.

We might not breathe as vampires but our reaction to pain and odd sensations in our bodies are the same. Jumping up at the male who is in a little bit of shock at hurting his sister, I land a kick to his sternum, his body convulsing forward as I stamp down hard on Velen's right leg straight after.

Holding strong, her leg rejects my stamp, her body healing in the throat far quicker than I thought it would. Flashing to her feet, she hits out at me, my own arms coming up to block each hit as they try to land.

Caught in the sequence of movements Velen is throwing at me, I kick out behind me at her brother again, his own body coming back into to play. Making my way under her punches, I hit Velen in the chest pushing her hard enough to fling her onto the roof next to us.

Flashing into an attack, Valdin surprises me by spinning around behind me and biting into my neck. Ripping the skin of as he tears it like a wolf would do, I drop forward, kicking both my legs up behind me to kick him off into the space behind us.

With no choice of being able to lose this fight, I pick myself up off the floor, and curl my fingers so my nails can be used at their sharpest angle.

Moving in together, the brother and sister do what they do best and attack as one, letting me have it easy until now. Both kicking out to my sides at the same time, they work as if they have one brain. Darting down, Velen moves to attack my legs, as Valdin attacks my face, pure aggression flying at me with their sharper than diamond nails. Both using movement to attack what they are going for, Velen stabs at my calf's, the pain of her nails digging in reminding me of the punishment I received long ago.

No longer chained with vampires viewing my pain, I go for Valdin first, having had enough of being stabbed and scratched for one lifetime. His arms trying their best to get at my face, I let my arms fall partly, allowing him time to come at me. Grabbing his arms as one goes for my face and the other goes for the healing bite mark on my neck; I yank him forward so he pushes Velen into my legs. Biting hard and rough, I go for Valdin's chest, aiming my bites at where his heart lies.

Making it through his leather jacket in one bite, he wears no top underneath making this attack easy for me. Realising what I am doing far too late, I rip into Valdin's chest, his ribs breaking easily under the strength of my teeth. Feeling far stronger than a three hundred year old vampire, I rip into Valdin's body like it is a bread roll, chewing into his body so quickly I have his heart in my mouth before Velen can even see what is happening to her oddly quiet brother.

Not giving Valdin the one chance of escape, I bite into his heart, his body turning instantly to dust as I do. Power and rage flowing through me, I know what I have just achieved shouldn't be possible with a vampire against vampire. Even

Volmir would have struggled to bite on through another vampire's chest while holding them still.

Screaming her brother's name, I see red as I dive into Velen's heap of a body below me, her brother's ashes covering her entirely. Grabbing her arms by each wrist, I pull at them yanking them away from her body in such a rage. The vile creature that tortured me will now pay her price. No cousin of mine, I rip her arms off her body, her deep sapphire tinged blood pouring out onto the roof.

Given up by her brother's true death, I grab under Velen's chin. Using her body as a counter, I step one foot onto her chest, ripping at her neck. Pulling hard, I dig my nails in as I ripe skin from skin, bones from bones, as every muscle in her neck contracting, her true death coming onto her waiting soul as I pull her head from her body.

Turning to ash, the moment her head comes clean off, I fall backwards the momentum of my strength making me stumble hard. Falling back, I didn't realise I was on the edge of the building, my body falling down to the hard empty street that Volmir just died in.

Landing with a crack, my body dents the cobbles, a hole forming where I lay. Covered in ash and sapphire blood, I feel my neck knitting back together, my soul not wanting to move for a moment. I have just killed my punishers, just watched the monster than ruled for an unfair treatment of me, ruled the vampires wrong, just get murdered by a united human front.

All of this has happened, but I know my task is still not done. The evil hunting me is still out there and I cannot wait for it to come to me. Rising to my feet, I dip into my pockets, the sage still there managing to protect me from the grey cloud's gaze.

Feeling the small orb waiting for me still, I pull it out, bringing it up to show me which way I need to go. With my new found strength and rage disappearing throughout my partly hurt body, I begin walking, using this new found power to hunt the evil coming for me.

Ten

A cottage, broken down, desolate stands before me, its coldness left to the natural world. This place, a simple house means its owner cannot be anyone of note. As sad as it seems to say, this house and its occupant are not anyone special, so why has this orb brought me here.

Maybe that's the game they are playing or even worse, the orb isn't leading me to where I want to go at all. Maybe the orb is broken, or the Pagan with all his power has led me down to my own death, one that has nothing to do the grey cloud.

Out of the city limits, I'm now in a small town half a mile to the closest main roadway. With a common thatched roof, the place is even painted a colour that surprises me.

Grey, like the cloud of fog seeping out of the gaps around the front door, the colour is one no-one of this time would choose to go for. Cold in its exterior, the cottage's windows have been painted from the inside to keep any light out. The garden, which I'm sure was very nice once, has now become a broken mess. Unkempt, nature has claimed back the land it was once ejected from, the path made of gravel being the only thing to have survived natures firm grip.

My right hand holding the small orb strong, its grey glow is flaring brighter the more I stand in front of this house. In my left hand, I grasp my sage protector tightly, making sure I can protect myself long enough to last this encounter.

Two storeys, the cottage has four windows in the front, each one being only the size of a portrait painting. A two stumped funnel sticks out of the top left, where the grey cloud seeps out into the night air.

Oddly calm, I do not feel the fear that has gripped me the last few days. Unsure if it is because I am finally here, or after my win, I foolishly feel braver in myself to fight this evil. Having had enough of waiting, of wonder what this evil is I move, deciding my best way inside is through the back.

Flashing to the side gate, I speed through the overgrown front garden; making my entry into this house with as much speed as I can. Rather than unlatching the gate and trying to push against the overgrown grass in the back garden, I grab hold of the brick archway above me and swing myself over like a gymnast. With ease and grace, I feel as if I am sort of flying, my fear for this evil echoing in my head.

Feeling so good for finding this creature so quickly, the echo washes away my bubbling insecurities about how I am going to defeat this power. If I have made it this far without a problem, finishing the job should be very easy.

Covered by the trees circling the whole of the outer edge of the garden, the moon's natural light is no help here for any mortal. With my perfect eyesight, even in the darkest of places, I scan the area, listening for anything in the house.

Completely dead inside of noise, the overgrowth looks eerie, as if the presence of death has taken over.

A rotten table with a half broken swing-chair is covered in moss, nature having claimed every inch of this land back. Clearly the main feature of this space, the garden seems like its own secret from the town spread out here. Not as close together as the buildings in the city are, this town still has its houses closer together. Meaning the regular citizens of this town must see how bizarre this place is, unless the grey cloud can create illusions just like the pagan does with his home.

Taking a step forward, I hear a shuffle in the brush, the movement of whatever made the noise, is swishing some of the grass just ahead of me. Moving so slowly, I feel as if I am not moving at all, the grass tickles at my skin like a lost friend who hasn't seen you in a while.

The grass having grown over whatever has moved, as I slink closer I see it isn't movement at all in the brush. Instead, before me is a set of family bones, four human sets to be exact. Grown around and through the old bones, moss and the grass have transformed the bones into nature's own work of art. The moss covering the white structures, give the bones a fantasy look that many try to add to new statues they put up.

Seeing the reason for the movement of the brush, grass stems rustling against some of the bones when the wind blows past knocks against others making it seem as if a creature is hiding to pounce. Feeling everything tenfold, even this slight negative energy, I feel nothing can get past me, when I am on high alert like tonight.

Piled on top of one another, the bones all look as if they have been beaten. All adults, the bones feel to me that there were two older than the others but they were all killed the same way. Night creatures kill by sucking the blood out of their victims, draining them dry. The fact that these victims were drained of all their blood before they died, meant the rate of decomposition was rapid. Drying out fair quicker than someone who has their blood, the darker shade on the bones informs me of how they died.

Giving me no evidence that this great evil I am following has anything to do with this; I turn away from the bodies and look to the back of the cottage.

The same as the front, the cottage has painted out windows, meaning whoever is inside is afraid of being seen. Clearly not my kin, any vampire wouldn't need to block out the sun with paint, a heavy set of curtains is good enough.

I may not know everything a vampire can do, but I know this grey cloud is not something someone of my kind can do. Hiding, like this evil is, I know whoever killed these humans are long gone, but thanks to them I can enter this home without the worry of needing permission from anyone of magic to enter. With the rules on entering a home being different with each individual house, I can feel by the power coming off this house that no power will stop me entering.

A broken window in the top left; I see no escaping grey cloud, meaning that this is my entry point. Flashing to the bottom of the wall, I glance one more time at the empty garden, checking no one is sitting out here hiding in waiting for me to start climbing.

Having won the fight against two of my kind and after the ritual the pagan performed, I do not think I can take much more on this night before facing this evil. Being here means I must face it, otherwise I may not get another chance.

Raising one hand to the wall, I sink my nails into the hard crust covering the bricks beneath. Stabbing in deep, I wait for my fingers to find the stonework, making sure I have just the right amount of resistance to fight against my rising weight. Keeping the two objects in my hands, I feel safer with the sage touching my skin.

Climbing up some buildings with such an ease it is like I am not even touching them, cottage homes are a different matter. Knowing the weight of the stonework beneath and the paint above it, I cannot help but feel the pressure that I could easily smash through the wall. Making sure I do not let the evil within know I am here, my only way of winning will be with surprise.

Moving myself up the wall as I go, I turn my hearing to the interior of the building. Silence beyond my own, I feel nothing from inside. No bodies, no person, not even power. The pain in my head, the shakes of my own body every time I have gotten close to this grey cloud, I feel none of it as I make it to the window.

Knowing the power of this sage is strong; I know it is not strong enough to numb the clouds power completely. Closing my eyes, I give it one last listen, this one being the final test before I move in fangs sharpened.

A creaking sound comes from deep within making me shift my weight as power calls out to me. Dipping my head so it lays on the bumpy surface, I tweak my ears, trying to learn what is going on inside.

Another creak, closer this time, I move so one hand hangs on the inside of the home, the protection of someone alive and owning this house long gone.

Feeling the vibes, any vibes I can, I hear a third creak further away from the first two.

Taking a risk, I lift myself up and into the cottage, the outside world and all its jumbled noise ceasing as I do. Empty and hollow, every piece of furniture and fixtures has been taken from this room, leaving an empty shell of hatred in its wake.

A creak breaking, I snap to my right, the sound coming from the other side of the wall ahead of me. No breathe or heart beats, I wonder if this evil exists at all. Maybe this whole time the grey cloud is just cleansing this world of my kind. Maybe it's here to take out every last one of us because the holy one has listened to its subject's prayers. Maybe I feel nothing here because I am alone in this house. The divine grey cloud is here waiting for my kind to come to it, not the other way around.

Needing answers, I wait, listening for one last creak of the floor boards in this empty shell that once was a home.

Deafening, the growing silence of my need to hear something again, rises up inside me. My self-doubt and fear circling its way back into my body, I feel a slight shake entering my left hand, the sage in it losing its hold against this evil.

Doing the only thing that feels right, I bring the small orb up, its tiny grey surface screaming at me with a bright glow for being inside.

Waiting only a moment more to see if any sound sparks, my fingers itch at wanting to do something. Not like a normal hunt, my patience and hunger are gone, the need to get this over with is fuelled by the fear creeping its way back in. The fear overpowering me, I feel my arm rise up, the orb leaving my hand breaking contact with me as the fear takes over me entirely.

Slipping from my fingers in a throw of anger and hate, the orb sails through the air aimed for the spot I last heard a creak.

Small as it is, but the orb contains a vast amount of power, both a darkness, light and the grey cloud, the protective seal being the only thing holding it together. Shattering in a loud earthquake of sound, the orb breaks apart its whole marble exterior easily.

My own body flying forward as the orb hits it mark, I am pulled into the orbs shattering skin, the fighting powers escaping in one moment, rip down all the walls in the room like they never existed. Opening up the rest of the house to me; the powers inside the orb scratch at me, using me as a plaything for their fight. Raw and real, the powers call out to me from both my ears and my mind, my soul feeling as if it is connected to both of them.

The ritual I performed with the pagan, having a more of an effect on my mind and soul than I thought, I feel a warm touch caress my shoulder as I am yanked back against the wall I came in through.

Horns and hope stare at me from the front now, the god who helped with the ritual appearing to me once more. Nodding his head at me for a response, it itself is pulled back into the raging powers fighting away in this hollow cottage.

"Thank you…" I question, wondering if that is what he wants. A thank you for saving me from this power I have unleashed or an apology for smashing the orb containing his magic, I do not know.

Feeling drawn to the powers still fighting where I stood only a second before, the pagan's magic hits out at me, the god vanishing once again. Slapping me in the face, I feel the hot and cold of the two forces, both battling to gain control of the now emptied area I am trapped in.

Returning once more like an arch angel, the god holds his hands out from the other side of the room, drawing his divine power back into his own body. Taking what hope I have left in this space, I feel the sage being taken from my grip, the god using his own magic to separate me from my protector.

"You are the evil?" I shout wondering how I could have missed this.

Shaking his head, the god pulls at his power sucking all the good he was feeding into the world back into himself, even taking Amara's pagan magic with him. Yanking at the sage, I feel the herb leave my grasp; the feeling of it happening just like when I threw the orb, my body not actually doing it because I want too.

Why would this god, this being want to destroy my kind. Helping the pagan surely didn't help him feed his grey cloud to the world; it's drew me here, right into his arms.

Understanding my mistake, how could I think this supposed god and his pagan were helping me, when this was the plan all along. Bringing me to the place where the power is strongest and I will be taken off their list of needing to be caught. I have just opened myself up to it instead.

"Why do you want to kill all of my kind!" I shout at him, wanting at least one answered question before I lose.

Shaking his head again, he motions to the space around us, his arm still moving as it is the last thing I see before he takes all of his light out of this realm.

Grey clouds everywhere, I cannot believe I have been so naive. First I think this would be easy, I will come here and kill whatever I need to. Next I will destroy every ounce of grey this world now has in it and live my life how I want it. How could I think a god was behind all of this. Understanding the last motion of his arm, I see now his last warning that I need to stop looking for blame and await my fate.

Letting myself relax, I drop from the pressure of being held against the wall, my expectance of my fate clearly being the reason the god has let his vice grip on me go.

Just like in my dreams, the grey cloud seeps towards me; forming two hands of out of the fog. Growing even thicker, the deeper the colour gets the harder the fog seems to become. Creeping closer and closer I see my fate before me, my mind screaming as the presence calls out to me.

Seeping into my head like it did in my dreams and at the front gate, I turn from the cloud, making one last effort to escape this fate I do not want. My hands smashing out before me, I break all the glass of the cottage window, my flashing speed kicking in as I make my move to flee.

Soft gentle fingers caress my temples as the grey cloud imbues its power fully onto me. My last effort gone, I see flashes of the outstretched hands coming for me from my dreams, the same fingers now pressed against my head forever taking me away.

Letting out the loudest scream I can manage, I feel the feral beast rising up to take hold of my soul, my true self disappearing...

Cayden McNigh returns in...

The Feral Night Creature

Enjoy The Sleepless Night Creature?

Leave a review Online

Follow **HDA Pratt**
On Instagram **@hdapratt** or
Follow the **HDA Pratt author page** on facebook.
Keep up to date with all of HDA's latest news on his website

Worthy

Book one in The Elemental Cycle

HDA PRATT

Prologue

Terra

Not a cloud in sight above her dreadlocked head, Terra knew. Knew that the first full day of summer had finally arrived and the sun was granting them, the newly unemployed friends the perfect weather. Complementing the elation running through her soul, Terra's warm laughter rings out at the sight of her dog being bested by the brute that is Eline's beast.

Lika's bronze fur catching the light of the sun so perfectly; it reflects a shine any freshly polished armour would be jealous of. With her brute force and German Shephard descent, Lika is not a dog to be messed with. Master of the uncontrollability Lika, Terra cannot help secretly liking the fact that her soothingly calm best friend Eline holds the power of taming such a beast.

Crushing soft sand between her toes, Terra lets the riverside's beauty sink in. Looking to her friends, she notices the weight-fullness that they all shared, has vanished. After one simple act, one of defiance, of not living a life placed upon them. All it took was to throw away what was expected and embrace their deserved freedom.

Jumping to her feet, water rushes at her and Eline, soaking her giant friend's legs. Kicking the water at Eline, a look of mischief covers the Dutch woman's face, her revenge ensuing. Giving off a screech that could only match that of a mountain lion's roar, Eline drags Terra back down into the liquid. Watching their owners copy their play fighting, the two dogs jump into the water, attacking the giggling girls.

Splashes and barks echoing down the river's water that for today was somehow blue. A warm breeze blowing under the arching bridge high above, it throws itself at the drenched group. Laughing down at them, Terra sees Donald watching from above; happy he chose to not sit at the water's edge. Distracted by him, Terra feels her golden dreads soak up a massive amount of water from Eline splashing a wave over her.

Helping each other up, they move out of the water quickly, having had enough of being in the murky Suffolk water. The only one unhappy to leave it, Eline's puppy buzzes with constant energy, deciding in a second that she is finished with Terra's Maggie, Lika barrels herself at Donald. Licking his face, the dog pins him on his back, over-powering him easily.

Stretching to the height of six foot two, Terra was sure Donald had not stopped growing even after making it to the age of twenty-two. Combined with his build, Donald could easily hold back the power of Lika, if he truly tried. His pale skin and ever-changing green eyes show the English/Scottish mix that his parents created. With a round shaped face, his neatly trimmed beard tinged by a ginger glow, hides his baby fat beneath. Shaved to one length, Terra thinks how much older her handsome friend looks with his brown hair clipped to its new style.

Laying down a few feet away from the attacking puppy, Terra's Maggie watches the younger pup fire a constant stream of energy at Donald. Rubbing Maggie's wrinkly head, a pair of watery eyes shines out from the droopy skin that has dropped with Maggie's ever growing age. With her puppy-like spikes of energy dwindling, Terra can't help but wonder how many years her boxer has left.

"Nee Lika" Eline shouts in her native tongue, clicking her fingers. Hearing Eline use her first language of Dutch, it sparks an ever-recurring reminder that her best friend originates from Holland. Apart from the tang in her accent and that she towers even above Donald; Terra always forgets that fact about her. Two years they've known each other and the only question about Holland Terra had had been short and sweet. Did Eline think in Dutch or English.

"Nee Lika" Looking to her owner, Lika's ears flop down, her eyes turning a pure black as she contemplates her next move. Holding back a smile, Terra watches the power struggle between master and canine. Clicking her fingers as one last warning, Lika gives a last ditched effort at licking Donald.

"Heir Lika" Eline calmly speaks her words, pure strength and no anger coming off of her. Scolded, Lika slowly shuffles over to Eline's side, before thumping herself into a seated position. Glancing at Maggie, her tongue hangs out as she showers her in a loving gaze. Thanking the heavens Maggie was never like that as a puppy, she pats her girl's soft head.

"Thank you. I thought she was going to lick me to death." Donald chuckles.

"I still can't believe we did it guys." Squeezing water out of her dreads onto the sand, Terra changes the subject. "I cannot stop thinking about it." Splashing some water in front of her bare chocolate coloured feet, a few droplets sprinkle onto Maggie's head, making her scamper away in irritation.

"It felt exhilarating didn't it" Donald beams.

"Exhilarating" Eline repeats. "It was one of the best decisions I could have ever made!" She shouts gaining a bark from Lika.

"Seeing the look on Red's face, I wish I had filmed it. Just so I could see the way her mouth fell open in utter surprise." Terra laughs, so happy she will not have to see the patronising girl ever again.

"CCTV would have picked it up if the cameras were facing in the right direction." Donald states, taking his name badge off his now unneeded uniform. "If only it hadn't been in the moment, we could have set up hidden cameras. Being able to see that for the rest of my life would have been priceless."

Copying him, Terra rips her brown square shaped name badge off and leans forward to the sandy part of the riverside. Creating a hole in the sand, she places her broken badge inside. "Come on guys let's keep walking. I still have so much energy to burn."

Joining Terra, her friends drop their badges in the hole before she smothers the sand back over. Grabbing their shoes, they whistle to get the dogs on track and start walking again.

"We should continue this feeling and go on an adventure" Donald puts out there.

"What kind of adventure?" Eline asks. "Though you know I'm definitely down for an adventure anytime" She adds quickly.

"I don't know something with a kind of goal to reach." Donald thinks aloud. "Maybe-" Clicking his fingers, Terra sees the light go on inside. Certain she knows what he's going to say, he proves her thoughts right. "Let's walk the Great Wall of China."

"You and that bloody wall." Terra chuckles "China's quite a way to go. Let's start smaller by walking to Shotley first." Unsure if a huge adventure is what she wants; Terra picks up the pace of her walk.

"We don't have to go to China. I just want to -" Spinning on the spot he shouts. "Go somewhere!" Arms raised he acts like he's in a movie by dropping to his knees for dramatic effect.

"Oh god" Terra huffs

Shocking Donald out of his acting scene, Terra huffs gaining an odd look of disgust from Donald, before he realizes she isn't looking at him. Seeing the approaching figure coming their way, Terra knew this is karmas way of payback.

"Shall we run?" Donald suggests

"No, I want to see his reaction when we tell him what happened." Eline's eyes bulge at the thought of shocking Sirel.

"Imagine if he had been there as it had unfolded." Laughing aloud, Terra pictures the man's already red face, burning as bright as Red's overly dyed hair.

From the first time she served the approaching figure, he seemed to have some sort of radar of when she was out walking Maggie. Always bringing with him the monster that is his bosses' dog, it would always go for her boxer. Out for a leisurely stroll on his own, Terra couldn't help instinctively looking to see if the odd customer had brought the horse-sized dog like usual.

Working for a very well respected Suffolk council member, Sirel's boss had family money running back to before the wheel was invented. Ignoring her whenever he came into the shop, Sirel only had a soft spot for Donald. Never having anything in his own life when he came into the shop, Sirel only came in with a list from his boss. Sadness emanating around him, wherever he goes, the loneliness is soon understood whenever he decides to speak to them. Although being a groundskeeper for his boss's estate, working alone must be enough for him.

Unfortunately, disliking him comes easily for Terra. Based on his views of life and how he speaks of many people, her dislike is understood but the way he treats Eline and her, it pushes her hate even higher. Coming from Ireland his annoyingly toned voice hasn't kept any of the Irish pleasantries. In fact, he has completely lost his accent, though what is left is a squeak that scraps its way out of his throat.

Wearing his signature dark green fishing coat, it hangs like death around his knees. Covered head to toe, she's confounded that the heat of the sun doesn't make him pass out.

"Ah Donald" He squibs

Looking at the group in turn, he passes over Terra for a greeting, but not before managing to give a dirty look at Maggie. Bitterness towards the man rising inside her, she turns her face into a dirty look of her own.

"Dutch girl, fantastic weather we're having. Shame you're not sailing along the river." He motions at the calm water. "Is your boat every going to be finished?" Without taking a breath he continues, cutting her off before Eline can answer.

"I don't doubt when it is finished, you won't make it far" Bursting out in a fit of laughter, his pleasure at his insult is clear.

"Hello Sirel" All three friends chime together, biting back their hate.

"Are you not hot in your coat?" Terra asks.

"Hot?" A puzzling look crosses his face. "No, the breeze sends a chill right through me, I cannot stand the wind." Answering Terra question to Donald, Terra watches with happiness that a flush of red heats his face giving away his lie.

"Oh, that's a shame. I was about to say you could come for a ride on my boat now it's finished." Pointing out onto the river, Eline shows Sirel where the Reis floats upon the water.

"But the wind will definitely be blowing when my Reis sets off."

Sparkling clean, the top shines white in the sun while its bright red underbelly bops in the cloudy brown water. Unlike Sirel who only glances, Terra makes out the design of a mystical creature stretching the length of the boat, designed by one of Eline's many talent friends. The boats name coming from Eline's own language, it means journey, Terra's mind releasing maybe Donald's idea isn't a bad one after all. Maybe somehow they were always meant to have the events happen today; maybe Eline somehow foretold an adventure to come by naming the boat Reis.

"It looks so clean Dutch girl"

"And why wouldn't it be?" Donald asks

"Well, you're from another country so you can never tell" Sirel says contradicting his own origin.

"You are just a dick aren't you?" Donald snaps his pretence of liking this man is truly gone now he no longer has a job to keep.

Taking Terra by surprise, the anger in her friend's voice matches the devil. Understanding Sirel was no longer a customer, she still couldn't believe he really just shouted at the old fool.

"Seriously what is wrong with you?" Donald raises his voice "Firstly you can't even register Terra's existence. Then you never call Eline by her name, as you clearly can't be arsed to learn it. All you seem to be able to do is make rude snarky comments about her boat and country. How old are you six? Even a six year old wouldn't be so rude to people!"

"I don't get it Sirel, you yourself are from another country" Eline adds

"Holland is a forward-thinking country. Way more than the one I'm standing in with you around"

"Donald you should-" Terra begins but Donald turns on her.

"What! I shouldn't finally tell this insolent man what we all think of him. I've had enough"

Taking a step back Sirel looks shocked, still not understanding what he's done wrong. Motioning for Donald to continue Terra hopes her angered friend is nearly over.

"Being respectful of someone, means you don't have to say every horrible thought that comes into your head. It's someone who knows not to say something at all. I so hope I never have to see you again Sirel... have a great day" He finishes, signing off like he is at work.

Storming pass the man, Donald heads up the water's edge whistling for the girls dogs to follow. Giving Maggie the nod her boxer is waiting for, the dogs run off after the angered man. An awkward silence following Donald's rant makes Terra look to the Reis wondering if she could swim out to it. If it wasn't for the horrible water stuck between them, her and her friends could already be sailing the seas.

"What did Donald mean by never seeing me again?" Still oblivious to anything her friend said she wants to shake the fool.

"You won't see us on the deli anymore," Eline says "None of us in fact."

"Ah! Why will I not?"

"We no longer work at the shop!" Done with the conversation Terra snaps. Pushing her tall friend in Donald's direction, she gives the old man a final look.

"I'm sure you'll hear all about it next time you go in." Eline says over her shoulder "Goodbye Sirel"

Worthy

by
HDA Pratt

A Magical Creature Series

Book one – Flighty: a magical creature novella is about a fairy who cannot not fly like the rest of his kind. Sent on a journey by his mermaid friend Nerdiver, book one is this series is about a fairy finding the courage to become the creature he is destined to become or will the power of others change his and his homelands world forever.

Book two – Nerdiver: a magical creature novella is a continuation of Flighty's journey; however this book concentrates on the life of Nerdiver, Flighty's mermaid friend. Trapped in a pond she has lived in all her life, one creature is about to come that may change all of that forever. Will Nerdiver choice freedom over duty? Or is freewill far more powerful into how one becomes the person they are meant to be.

Both books are available on amazon in Kindle or Paperback

Printed in Poland
by Amazon Fulfillment
Poland Sp. z o.o., Wrocław